ISLAND KISSES

A BILLIONAIRE LOVE STORY

KRISTA LAKES

ZIRCONIA PUBLISHING, INC.

ABOUT THIS BOOK

Harper Thomas loves bad dates. She goes on hundreds of them a year, and then blogs about them online to make her living. When her sister signs her up for a new dating service, Harper's not expecting to find anything other more than ridiculous men. She certainly isn't planning to meet *him*...

Gabe Honors is one of the billionaire owners of Kindling Dating. He also happens to be Miami's most eligible bachelor, but his search for love has never been successful. That is, until he decided to use his own dating service. The first time he meets Harper, he knew that she was the one. However, in order to make sure that it really was love, he kept his identity a secret. He soon finds out, secrets never mix well with love...

Can a billionaire CEO finally stump this bad-date-blogger? Can Harper look past the money and find the man? Or will they only be left with memories of their island kisses?

I looked out from one of the big windows overlooking the water. The sun was finally setting and from where we sat, I could see the sky outside as it began to turn orange. It looked to be a breathtaking sunset.

"Can we watch the sunset?" I asked, already standing up.

"Of course!" Gabe said, nearly knocking over his chair and taking my hand.

I followed him out to the patio and we stepped up to the railing. The ocean sprawled out in front of us, all the way to the horizon, where the sun sat lonely on the water. The sky was on fire, making the incredible view from the island even more breathtaking. A warm breeze blew off of the sea, causing my hair to fall across my forehead. Gabe reached over and pushed the loose hair over my ear. His touch was soft, as if he were afraid I might disappear if he touched me.

"You look beautiful tonight," he said. "Thank you for coming over for dinner."

I smiled as I stepped closer to him. "The food was wonderful. But I'm still pretty excited to try out your world famous Ramen noodles one of these days."

Gabe chuckled and then leaned in, surprising me with a kiss. The passion in the air ignited instantly as we embraced in front of the sunset. The island air blew through my hair, carrying with it the scent of saltwater and warm sand. It was a picture perfect moment; one that I never saw myself actually experiencing. This island kiss was the most romantic kiss of my life.

Gabe gently pulled away, just long enough to look at me with those glowing green eyes. Then he leaned in again. Our lips parted this time and the kiss became more passionate, with our tongues delicately dancing. My hands drifted up his back. I could feel the definition of his muscles, even over his shirt, and it turned me on even more. I wanted to feel his naked skin, his firm body, all of him and all at once.

This is what I've wanted for so long, I thought. *And I want so much more.*

It was as though he had heard my thoughts. Gabe slowly broke our kiss and then brought his lips to the outside of my neck. My jaw dropped and I let out a silent gasp as he kissed my sensitive skin, inching his way down toward my shoulder. My body was on fire now and a desperate aching presented itself in my most sensitive areas.

Gabe pulled away and looked at me. His eyes had dilated and there was an expression of animalistic lust on his face. He was breathing harder than before and when I glanced down, I noticed a growing bulge in the front of his slacks. No words were exchanged. There were none needed.

Everything that could have been said was written all over our faces and our body language. We wanted each other right then and there, and all of the time we had spent together so far had just been leading up to this magical moment.

"Kiss me," I whispered.

He did as I asked and brought his lips to mine once again. Sweet and hot, our tongues tangled together. Our inhibitions quickly faded, replaced by a relentless passion. It was almost as if I had lost control, submitting to my most carnal desires.

My hands drifted over his body. I loved the way his muscular shoulders flexed with even the tiniest of his movements. I couldn't get enough of his biceps either, which swelled as he pulled me close. Everything about this man turned me on.

After a moment, Gabe broke our kiss and then grabbed my hand, leading me across the porch to a lounging area that had a circle of padded patio furniture on it. In front of us, the sky had turned from orange into a shade of deep purple as the sun continued its decline behind the horizon. The stars were beginning to show and the night air cooled, though it was still comfortably warm.

"You're something else, Harper," Gabe commented. His eyes pupils dilated as he looked me over. "I can't put my finger on it, but there's something about you that drives me crazy. And I mean that in the best of ways."

I simply smiled coyly as I sat down on one of lounge chairs and patted the seat next to me. The bulge in Gabe's pants had grown significantly and was pushing out against the material. He wanted me. Just seeing that turned me on even more and caused the desperate aching inside of me to increase. I wanted what was underneath that cloth. I wanted it so badly.

Gabe crawled onto the padded lounger with me, pushing my shoulder with one hand and cradling my head with the other as he lay me down. He nipped at my exposed collarbone, dragging his teeth along the soft flesh and making me gasp with desire. The bottom of my dress shifted upwards as I wrapped my legs around him. It felt strange to be so exposed outside, but given that there was nothing but ocean in front of us, I wasn't worried about being seen.

Gabe paused in his kisses, pulling back for a moment and looking me over. His pupils dilated further. "You are so gorgeous," he whispered reverently.

I couldn't help but to blush at the compliment. I had been called gorgeous before, but when Gabe said it, it just *felt* different. There was such sincerity in him. It wasn't just in his voice, though. It was written all over his face too. He looked at me like he *needed* me in that moment and it made my insides turn to butterflies. All girls have their insecurities and I was no different, but when Gabe complimented me, it was like all of those things faded away. He truly made me feel beautiful.

After a second of admiring me, Gabe leaned in and kissed the top of my bare shoulder, causing pleasurable little goose bumps to pop up on my skin. I wrapped my legs around his waist and pulled him closer, feeling as his bulge pressed against the front of my panties. The friction sent of burst of pleasure into me and I moaned softly. The desperate craving inside of me begged for him, all of him.

"Gabe," I whispered, more to release the pressure building inside of me than to get his attention.

I wanted to tell him to take me right there, but I couldn't even get the words out. He had begun to grind his hips forward, increasing the friction and intensifying the pleasure.

Gabe moved his face downward toward my chest and kissed the top of my cleavage, letting out a lustful growl. My lips parted and I breathed in, pushing my chest upward and against his face. His skin was smooth with only a hint of stubble and I knew he must have shaved before I came over. My dress allowed him access to only a little bit of my cleavage, but I wanted him to have it all. I wanted his kiss all over my body.

"Let me take this off," I said, propping myself up on my elbows.

He held himself over me and then sat back. I quickly pulled the dress over my head, before tossing it onto a nearby lounge chair. Then I relaxed back into the cushion, sprawled in front of him in nothing but my bra and panties.

"Your turn," I ordered, with a sexual smile.

"I like when you tell me what you want," he replied, his mouth turning into a cocky smile. Gabe quickly unbuttoned his dress shirt. I watched as his chiseled chest and washboard abs were revealed.

You've got to be kidding me, I thought. *He's absolutely perfect. Better than perfect.*

He tossed the shirt to the side and the reached down to take off his belt. His muscles flexed as he moved and my jaw continued to drop. He was absolutely gorgeous. His skin was tan and his body was ripped. He looked more like an underwear model than he did a software engineer. While he took off his pants, I reached down and gently pinched the top of my thigh, just to make sure that I wasn't dreaming.

It turned out that I wasn't.

Gabe stripped down all the way to his gray boxer/briefs. He stood there at the foot of the lounge chair and I took in the view.

With my index finger, I used the "come hither" motion to get him back over. He obliged and resumed his position, hovering over me. Now that my dress was off, he had full access to my cleavage and he didn't hesitate to bring his mouth there, gently biting and kissing my sensitive skin.

Our bodies became entwined. I wrapped my legs around him and pulled him close, once again feeling the friction, though now there was even less cloth between us. My senses lit up and waves of pleasure pumped into me with each movement of our hips. While Gabe kissed my cleavage, I unclasped the front of my bra to fully release my breasts. He let out a sexual growl and then brought his mouth over one of my nipples.

I gasped as his flicked his tongue against the sensitive bud, causing it to grow firm in an instant.

"Yes..." I panted.

Gabe gently licked and nibbled on the top of my breasts, creating a combination of pain and pleasure that had my senses exploding. He focused on that for a moment and then brought his face to the other side of my chest to give equal attention to my other breast. I was in heaven. Total heaven. There was nothing else I wanted in the entire world in that moment, except for more of what Gabe was already giving me...

Don't forget to sign up for my newsletter! You'll be the first to see my new covers, comment on new books of mine, and always know when books are available for free or on sale!

ISLAND KISSES

CHAPTER 1

This was a predictably terrible first date.

I couldn't have been more pleased.

I checked my watch and sighed, waiting for him to come out of the bathroom so I could go home and write everything down about our horrible date.

Granted, he hadn't thrown up on me, no one had been mugged, my car was its original color, I didn't need a new haircut, and my shoes were still intact, so it wasn't going to make my list of Top Five Worst Dates Ever, but it was not going well.

Which suited me just fine.

First, he was late. He claimed parking trouble, but as I had found a spot in about thirty seconds and could see at least two spots from our table, I had a hard time believing that. I wouldn't have been as mad if he had just owned up to leaving late rather than making lame excuses.

He then spent the entire time talking about nothing but his *very* important job as mail clerk for a *very* important legal firm. Apparently, he was absolutely indispensable to the company, despite the fact that he'd worked there for three years and hadn't moved up the ranks at all. But, according to him, he was due for a promotion any day now.

Throw in the fact that he still lived with his mother, was staring openly at my chest, and his unwashed hair, it was the perfect example of a bad date. I was almost glad I couldn't seem to get a word in edgewise, as the more he talked, the more I was amazed at how bad our date was going.

I'd already learned six of his coworker's names and their entire work history before he gave me the opportunity to say what I did for a living. The moment really only came because he was too busy adding an entire block of cheese to his salad. When I brought up that I was a writer, he asked if I wrote those super popular vampire books. I said no, and he honestly had looked disappointed.

Yup, because an author that rich and famous with tons of Hollywood contacts would be using a free dating service and going to overpriced strip-mall Italian restaurants on a Wednesday night, I had wanted to say. Instead, I kept my mouth shut and just ate my salad instead. He went back to talking about the mail cart. I didn't mention that I didn't write books but that I wrote a successful dating blog and magazine articles instead.

It wasn't like I was going to get to say anything about it, let alone tell him my real writing dreams. Unless my boobs started talking, he wasn't interested in anything I had to say.

There was no chemistry, and, now, absolutely no conversation.

Well, it's hard to have a conversation when he spends the entire time in the bathroom, I thought to myself, checking my watch. So far he was at just over fifteen minutes in there. I understood that when you got to go, you got to go, but seriously? A first date at a nice Italian restaurant was not the place, especially when the check was sitting on the table.

"Anything else for you, miss?" the waiter asked, glancing at my date's empty seat and the equally empty check holder. I was ready to go home, and willing to pay to do it.

"Nope." I pulled out my credit card and handed it to him. "Just put it all on there."

At least that would let me get out of this stupid restaurant and go home. Mr. Bathroom, as I was going to call him in my next blog entry, needed to be written about. Even though the date had been terrible, at least I was going to get a good blog entry out of it. The fans of my blog, Never After Dates, would at least be entertained.

My torture was their entertainment.

I looked down at my watch again as the waiter dropped the check back with me. Nineteen minutes.

Don't worry, Dude, I telepathically said toward the men's bathroom, *I already got the check. You can come back now.*

As soon as he came back, I was out of here. I signed the check, noticing that he had ordered the lobster ravioli which cost twice what my spinach tortellini did. My credit card company was sure going to love me.

You'll just have to wait on those new shoes a few more weeks, I told myself. *Or write something really, really good.*

I didn't mind paying. I'm all for equal opportunity in the dating world. What irked me was that I wasn't asked about it. When he suggested we go to Luigi's, I had offered to go somewhere a little less pricey, but he had insisted.

Now, I could see why he had. He was the one getting the free meal.

I scowled as I signed the check with a flourish. My blog was relatively successful, but I was just squeaking by with my bills. I didn't need an eighty dollar bill out of nowhere when I normally had everything budgeted down to the last nickel.

I closed the check holder just as my date returned. He strolled up casually, as if he hadn't just missed over twenty minutes of our date by hiding in the bathroom. His hands weren't even damp. Either he took so long because he was drying them, didn't use the bathroom at all, or, *ew...*

"Thanks for getting that. Money's a little tight for me," Mr. Bathroom said, settling into his chair and taking a sip of his yellow soda. "How'd you like the food here?"

"It was as good as I've heard," I replied. I was trying not to be angry. If money was tight, we should have gone anywhere but Luigi's. Like I'd asked in the beginning. I stood up and smiled, picking up my purse. "It was nice meeting you, but I need to get going."

His eyes widened in surprise. "I thought you were going to come back to my place. My mom's out bowling tonight."

I blinked twice, not really sure how to respond to that. Where in the world had he gotten the idea that I was even remotely interested? I'd said all of three words the entire meal!

"Sorry," I finally managed to get out. "I can't."

He stared up at me like a lost puppy, but I wasn't about to fall for those eyes. It might work for his mom, but not for me. Especially after footing an eighty dollar meal after asking for a different restaurant. Luckily, he gave up quickly.

"Well, Hannah, it was really nice to meet you." He didn't get up from the table to offer me a hug or a handshake, and I was glad. I didn't want to touch him since I wasn't sure of the cleanliness of his hands.

"It's Harper. My name is Harper, not Hannah." I shouldered my purse and took a step back. "Have a great rest of the night."

"I'll call you!" he yelled out after me through the quiet

restaurant. The other patrons all stopped talking and stared as I walked by. Yup. This was a good date.

I simply waved and hurried out the front door as quickly as possible. Mr. Bathroom was going to make a great post for the Never After Dating series. Right up there with Mr. Small-Time Drug Lord and Mr. Ex-Con Drunk.

At least he hadn't puked on me.

"HEY, I'M ON MY WAY," I told my sister over the phone as I started the car engine. My ancient little Pontiac purred to life and I thanked my lucky stars. Some days she decided to drive like a dream, and on other days she was hell on wheels. Today would have been a terrible day for her not to start. There was no way I was walking back into that restaurant to get a jump start.

"How was the date?" Rosie asked.

"Awful," I said, pulling out onto the main road. "It'll be great for readers. I really think they're going to eat this one up."

I could hear her moving around on her end of the phone. "You're the only person I know who gets more excited about bad dates than good ones," she replied.

"Are you moving stuff around again?" I asked, ignoring her statement.

"No," she answered defensively before sighing. "Yes. Fine. I'm moving the crib to the other side of the room. I think the draft from the window will make him cold."

I couldn't help but smile. She was so excited for her first-born child that she had moved that darn crib at least six times in the last week. "You better figure out where to put it soon," I told her. "You've only got another month to figure it out."

"Oof-" She was obviously pushing the crib into place. "I know. I can't wait until I don't waddle anymore. I feel like a penguin."

"A cute penguin," I said, taking the next turn.

Rosie laughed. "That's what Thomas says, too." She panted slightly. I was going to have to tell her husband not to let her push that heavy stuff. Not that she'd listen to either of us, but it had to at least be said.

"Okay, well, I'll be there in about five minutes," I said, pulling off the highway and heading to her place. It was tradition to go see her after a failed date. Rosie had the best perspective and came up with the most epic tag lines for the blog entries.

"Oh good, you'll be here before Mom leaves," Rosie replied.

"Mom's there?" I asked. I nearly hit the brakes. It wasn't that I didn't like my mother. I loved her a lot. She just hated my blog, my love prospects, and what I was doing with my life. I could already feel the lecture.

"Is that you, Harper?" My mother's voice took over the phone. "I was just getting ready to go, but I'll wait until you get here. I brought the most adorable thing for the baby. You'll love it."

"Great, Mom." I wondered if banging my head against the steering wheel would make the airbag deploy. Then I could at least claim I got in an accident and I wouldn't have to explain to my mother, yet again, what I was doing with my life.

I pulled up to the house, making sure not to block my mother's exit in any way shape or form. I actually even parked on the opposite side of the street, just so that she could get out easier. Anything to help her leave as quickly as possible.

I didn't bother knocking. Thomas turned and waved from the living room as I walked in. He was a nerdy-looking guy, all elbows and knees, but he had a great smile. He wasn't my type, but he made my sister happy, so I loved him.

"Hey, Harper," he said. "How'd the date go? Awful, I hope?"

"Yup. It was perfectly terrible." I laughed, pausing by the couch to talk to him. "How's doctoring going? Not awful, I hope?"

He smiled. "I'm here and not at the hospital working, so things are good."

"Are you on call today?" I was stalling. I knew my mother and sister were in the baby's room, but I wasn't ready to face my mother just yet. Maybe I could just talk to Thomas until she had to leave...

"You can't avoid her forever." Thomas gave me a meaningful, *I know what you're doing and it's not going to work,* look. "And yes, I'm on call tonight. So don't swallow pennies or any other weird stuff tonight, okay? I want to stay home."

I chuckled. Thomas was a gastroenterologist at the local hospital. That was how he and Rosie met. Rosie was a radiology technician and the two had fallen in love over a barium x-ray. That was three years ago, and now they were expecting their first child in just a little over a month.

"You sure? Would swallowing pennies get me out of my mother asking me for the upteenth time why my love life is just a bad dates blog?"

Thomas looked thoughtful. "Nope. She'd probably just gown up and keep talking the whole way through your exam. And then she'd try and set you up with the first male nurse that walked in the door."

I shook my head and chuckled. That would be exactly what my mother would do.

"Harper?" My mother had heard us.

"On my way." I looked at Thomas. "If you hear screaming, don't come in. Just be prepared to help bury a body."

"Yours or hers?" Thomas asked.

"I'm not sure. It depends on who grabs the lamp first."

"Okay," Thomas agreed. "Just don't use the cute baby elephant lamp. I like that one."

"No baby elephant lamp, got it."

I started walking to the baby's room, feeling my shoulders tense up. I told myself to stop it. Maybe this time Mom wouldn't comment. Maybe this time she'd just show me whatever cute baby thing she'd found. Maybe she wouldn't bring up the fact that my younger sister had a real job, a husband, and a baby, while I was writing fluff pieces and wasting my life.

Maybe.

"There you are, Harper," my mom said as I walked into the baby's room. "I was beginning to think you forgot where the baby's room was."

"Nope, just talking to the baby daddy," I replied, going to give my sister and mother each a hug. "So, what did you bring?"

"Isn't it adorable?" My mother held up a little onesie with suspenders and a bow tie printed on it. To be fair, it was absolutely adorable. "I got one with a little tie, too."

I took the small outfit into my hands and studied it. It was so tiny. And cute. My nephew was going to be freaking adorable and the best dressed baby this side of the Atlantic.

"It's perfect," I replied, handing it off to Rosie. Rosie beamed. She looked amazing, even eight months pregnant. Her dark hair was pulled back into a ponytail and she was only wearing light makeup to accent her brown eyes, but she glowed. People always said we looked alike, and I hoped I looked half as beautiful as she did right now.

"So, when am I going to be able to purchase one of these for you?" Mom's question made my heart sink. We'd made it all of three minutes.

"Mom!" Rosie scolded. "Not cool."

"I'm just concerned about you, Harper." Mom pulled out the second onesie and put it on the changing table. "You just don't seem to be going anywhere."

"I'm going plenty of places, Mom," I told her through gritted teeth.

She put her hands on her hips and looked at me. It was easy to see where Rosie and I got our features. We all shared the same dark hair and eyes, a fairly average build, and noses that were probably just a little too big for our faces.

"You keep going on these terrible dates and not caring that you're not finding anyone. I know you just got back from another terrible one that you're super excited to share with the world. How are you going to find love like this?" Mom's features looked concerned, but I knew exactly the words that were coming next. "It's like you're not even trying, Harper."

Every time. Those words killed me every time. Because I was trying. The whole reason the Never After Dates even existed was because I was trying and not getting anywhere. It was making lemonade out of the lemon dates that life kept handing me.

The fact that I now hoped for bad dates had nothing to do with it. Now, it was part of how I paid my rent. I had found that lemonade could be profitable.

"I do write other things than this one dating blog," I

reminded my mother. "Just last month, I won the General Excellence award for my travel piece in *Now Magazine*."

"Yeah, but, honey, that isn't going to get you someone to love." My mother frowned. "I'm just worried about you and your future. I want you to be happy."

"I was happy until about three minutes ago," I said quietly. My mother glared at me. I did my best not to roll my eyes. "I have plans. I have aspirations and I'm not hopeless, okay? I'll find someone when I'm ready."

There was a moment of silence. You'd think a woman who spent so many years unhappily married would at least be willing to support a child who wasn't even bothering with the notion of marriage at the moment, rather than push for intense focus on finding the right one.

"You're not getting any younger, Harper," Mom scolded. "I don't want you to end up wasting your life going on these terrible dates and ignoring the possibility of finding actual happiness someday. You're just sabotaging yourself."

"Right, Mom. I do this all so I can be miserable and alone. I want to end up as a crazy cat lady." I stalked over to the baby elephant lamp. It was a good thing Thomas made me promise not to use it, because it was incredibly tempting to throw it at my mother's head at the moment.

"Harper, she just wants you to be happy." Rosie said softly. She was always the peace-maker.

I didn't say anything. The only things I wanted to say, I knew I'd regret because they weren't nice. I really wished I got along as well with Mom as Rosie did, but Rosie was the golden child. She'd always done everything right. I was the screw up.

Rosie cleared her throat. "But, at least you have that really promising date coming up, right?"

"Of course I do," I replied automatically. Technically, every date was a really promising one. For my blog.

"You do?" My mom looked skeptical. "A good date or a bad date?"

"A good one," Rosie assured her. "A real, positive, find love kind of date. She's trying out this new dating service by Kindling Dating. They have this brand new application that's basically guaranteed to find your true love. And she has a date through it."

"I do?" I looked at Rosie and she widened her eyes to tell me to play along. "Oh, right. I do. I totally do."

"Sure." Mom crossed her arms. "Who is he?"

"A local business owner," Rosie answered. "And super cute. He likes football and has a great sense of humor. He's basically perfect for Harper."

"Is that so?" Mom did not look convinced. She glared at me again. "Why didn't you say anything?"

"Well, I... um..." I had no answer because I didn't know what the hell Rosie was even talking about.

"She didn't want to get your hopes up, Mom," Rosie interjected. "You get so excited for every single date she goes on, like she's going to get married next week if she finds the right one. That's hard to deal with."

I wasn't sure whether to strangle or hug my sister. On the one hand, a good date would get my mother off my back, but on the other, I had no clue what Rosie had planned. If there was no actual guy, Mom was going to be even more trouble than usual. I'd heard of this Kindling Dating, but as it cost money and actually advertised yielding good dates, I had stayed far, far away from it. My business was bad dates.

What the heck was my sister doing?

"Is this true, Harper?" My mother fixed me with her best mom glare. When I was a kid, I would confess to anything under that look. It was hard not to break down even though I was twenty-six years old and no longer living under her roof.

"Rosie wouldn't lie, Mom," I answered. It was true enough that I would avoid showing my guilty face.

Mom looked back and forth between the two of us for a moment before smiling broadly at me. "You have a real date?"

"Apparently," I said while Rosie nodded vigorously.

"I can't tell you how happy that makes me, Harper." Mom actually looked relieved. "I just want you to find that special someone and settle down like your sister. I need more grandkids and Rosie's baby needs some cousins."

"That's the plan, Mom. Date this guy, marry him, have lots of babies," I said, ticking off fingers for each item of my future.

"Don't be sarcastic, Harper," Mom scolded, but then she wrapped me up in a big hug. "I'm just so proud of you for trying."

Because I wasn't trying before, I wanted to say, but I kept my mouth shut.

"See, Mom, everything will work out," Rosie promised.

I looked over at her and she grinned with two thumbs up.

"Okay." Mom let me go and stood up straight. There were tears of joy in her eyes. If I had known that promising her a good date would make her this happy, I would have done it a long time ago.

"You okay, Mom?" I asked.

"I'm great, honey." She wiped her eyes and smiled. "I'm just so happy to hear you're actually going to give this one a chance. Please, give him an actual chance? Don't make him hate you like do with all the guys you go out with now."

I managed not to let my jaw hit the floor. "Yes, Mom."

"I have to get going," Mom announced. She hugged Rosie, then dropped to her knees to kiss Rosie's belly. "Be good in there, little one. You keep growing, you little cutie."

"Drive safe, Mom," I said.

"I will." She stood up from the floor and then gave me a big hug. "Thank you for trying this time, Harper. I love you girls so much."

"We love you too, Mom," Rosie assured her. I nodded.

"You didn't park me in, did you?" Mom asked, picking up her purse

"Of course not. You're free to go," I informed her. She smiled and waved and headed out the door. I could hear her saying goodbye to Thomas in the living room as she went and as soon as I heard her car engine start, I let out a huge sigh of relief.

"Well, that was fun," Rosie commented.

"Yeah." I turned to face her. "Especially the part where I have a date from Kindling Romance? What the heck was that, Rosie?"

"I should probably explain..." Rosie blushed.

"Yeah, that would be good," I agreed. "Please tell me how I have a date lined up at a service I never signed up for."

It was a lucky thing my sister was pregnant. I couldn't kill a pregnant lady.

CHAPTER 2

"*K*indling Dating?" I rounded on my sister as she put the cute onesie away into a closet full of onesies. "Did you really sign me up for Kindling Dating or was that just a way to get Mom off my back?"

Rosie didn't answer right away. She took her time putting the new clothes into the closet and then turned to face me.

"You really are signed up and you really do have a date," she finally said. "If you want it. No pressure."

"No pressure?" I flopped into the rocking chair, nearly flinging myself right back out of it. "You told Mom. She's going to follow up on this until I marry the the poor guy!"

Rosie frowned, her hand going to her swollen belly and pushing as the little boy inside of her kicked her like I wanted to do. "I thought it would be good for you. I thought you'd be happy."

"You signed me up for a dating service, Rosie," I said, trying to calm myself by rocking. The motion was soothing, but I was still agitated. "One that costs money. There's a reason I stay on the free ones. I don't want you paying for this kind of thing. You have a baby on the way. I want you to buy booties, not booty calls. The reason I haven't tried this one is that it's so expensive."

Rosie sighed and leaned against the wall. "I know. But the advertisements are so awesome! I'm trying to help you out."

"You're supposed to be the good one. Signing me up for dates without my knowledge is not good." I pressed my fingers into the bridge of my nose. "Maybe we can still get your money back..."

Rosie's lip quivered. "I really was just trying to help."

"Don't cry, Rosie," I pleaded. I knew her hormones were causing emotional swings. The last thing I wanted to do was make my baby sister cry because she was trying to help me.

"I'm not," she said with a sniffle. "And I already paid for it. It was supposed to be a present."

She wrapped her arms around her and looked at the floor, looking like a chastised child. I knew she really did just want to help.

I stood up and wrapped my arms around her. "I'm not mad, Rosie. Promise."

Holding her like this, I was transported back in time. Back to when Dad was still alive and we were just little kids. Rosie and I would hear Mom and Dad arguing upstairs almost every evening. Their marriage was not a happy one, but they stayed together because it was the "right thing to do." Whenever their arguments would fill the house, I would hold little Rosie close and we'd whisper secrets and jokes to drown out the unhappiness upstairs. She would bury her face into my shoulder, just like she was doing now, and I would keep her safe. It was why we were so close now.

"I just want you to find somebody. I want you to be happy, and you know that I'm proud of you and your blog, but it isn't taking you where you want to go." Rosie held me tight, letting the words spill out without having to look at me. "You deserve so much more than these bad dates all the time."

"Oh, Rosie..." I sighed, but I didn't know what else to say.

"So, when I saw the ad for this matchmaking service based on science and guaranteed to help you find love, I couldn't stop myself. I signed you up." Rosie shrugged.

"What about the date part?" I asked, not letting go. As long as I had her like this, she would spill everything.

"That was kind of an accident," Rosie admitted. "I filled out all the questionnaires and profile questions like I was you. It wasn't that hard, and it was actually kind of fun."

"You pretended to be me?"

"How else was I supposed to sign you up? Anyway, after I did all that, a guy contacted me. I mean you. I mean, your profile," she amended.

"And you answered him?" I asked, horrified. The first rule of online dating was not to talk to just anyone, but knowing Rosie, she probably responded to every single request sent to the profile. This was going to be a disaster.

"He was cute!" she shot back. "Super cute. And funny. You'll like him I promise."

"Funny?" I pulled back so I could look at her face. Funny meant they had a conversation. "How do you know he's funny?"

Rosie refused to meet my eyes. "I chatted with him online."

"Rosie, you're married!" I exclaimed. "You were totally flirting with another man. Does your husband know?"

"Actually, he helped a little bit." She bit her lip, still refusing to look at me. "He actually does a really good impression of you."

"Rosie!" I couldn't believe this. I was going to have to kill her *and* her husband now. It was a shame.

"He's charming," she promised. "Just give it a try. I have a really good feeling about this, Harper. A really, *really* good feeling. Please?"

I sighed. That was really the only response I had. There was no way I could tell my pregnant, hormonal, baby sister *and* my mother that I wouldn't at least give the guy a shot.

"Fine." I crossed my arms. "But just one date. And if it's awful, I totally get to blog about it."

Rosie's face lit up like the Fourth of July. "Really? Oh, that's so great! You'll really like this guy, I promise."

"Just how much did you chat with him?" I asked, suddenly a little nervous. She seemed way, way too confident about him for just a simple online chat. My stomach was doing nervous flips just thinking about what I was getting myself into.

"Not that much..." Rosie trailed off and began to mess with her phone.

"Rosie, how much?"

"Here, just look at him," Rosie replied, handing me her phone instead of answering my question. The dating website was pulled up to my profile. The picture of me was from her birthday party last year. I looked happy. Not sexy or flirty or any of the other emotions I usually chose to display, but happy.

I scanned down to the chat logs. It looked like Rosie and her husband and chatted Mr. Perfect Match quite a bit. I groaned, knowing I was going to have to go through all the chat logs.

But, at least the picture of the guy was good. He was definitely attractive. His hair was dark and messy, as if he'd tried to tame it but the wind had just picked up right when the picture was taken. Green, piercing eyes the color of emeralds peered back at me from a smile that could light up a room. The photo was just a head shot, but even then, it looked like he worked out.

"He's cute in *this* picture," I told Rosie. "If that's even him."

Rosie rolled her eyes at me. "Oh ye of little faith."

"I'm the one who has been doing this for a living," I said. "Do you know how many guys have amazing pictures? All of them. Then, in person it turns out that it was them ten years ago. Or their roommate. Or the guy on their underwear package."

"Just meet him, okay?" Rosie stood before me and batted her eyelashes. "If he's terrible, then you get a great article for your blog. If he's not..."

"Then you get a great 'I told you so,'" I finished for her.

I sighed again and looked at the picture again. He was really cute.

"Fine," I promised. "Not like I have a lot of choice in the matter. Can you at least give me my user name and password so I can read through the novel you three wrote each other?"

"We did not write a novel!" Rosie replied, snatching her phone from my hands. "We just had a couple of very nice conversations. That's it."

"Sure." I gave her a nice smile. "User name and password?"

"HarpStrings and GonnaFindMeSomeLUV!23," Rosie rattled off, emphasizing the capital letters. At least she had picked a decent password. I wasn't so sure on the user name, but it was too late now. Rosie chewed on her lower lip as she unconsciously rubbed her belly. Her dark brows were pulled together in fear that I'd still be mad. "Are we okay?"

"Of course we're good," I assured her, pulling her in for another hug. "I'm not terribly pleased, especially since you let Mom in on your little secret, but your heart was in the right place."

"Okay." Rosie smiled and then let out an excited gasp. "He's kicking."

She grabbed my hand and put it on her belly. It took a moment, but then I felt it. The life inside of her pushing and stretching, saying hello to the world outside. How could I be mad when I had that under my hands?

"He's getting so strong," I murmured, lost at the awe of feeling life growing right under my fingers. "I can't wait to meet him."

"Me too." Rosie shifted slightly as the baby kicked hard. "You are about to have a lot of good men in your life, Harper."

"Well, at least one," I agreed quietly. For a moment, I hoped that I wasn't just talking about the baby.

CHAPTER 3

"And so it is, Mr. Bathroom shall be forever memorialized for his unique ability to use a toilet as refuge from paying the bill. Ladies be warned; if you get picked up by a guy whose meal costs more than what he pays for rent, abort mission. Flee the scene. Leave before he comes back from hiding. At least today we know he gets to go back home to his mommy- let's just all hope she preps him a little more before his next date."

My arms fell from the keyboard as I allowed them a momentary rest. This was going to make for a great post, I could already tell. Posts like these came effortlessly with the most challenging part being accurately recalling the extent of the disaster. Every little detail was required to paint the full picture of what I had dealt with, and my readers ate it up.

As I was doing a final skim over the passage for any typos or grammatical errors, my phone buzzed obnoxiously on the table. I was usually good about not allowing my phone to distract me in the middle of writing, but because I was already mostly finished I allowed my eyes to steal a look at the notification that had popped up. It was a text message from Rosie.

I took a break to open the message and immediately regretted my decision. Her text was all of one sentence that I should have anticipated.

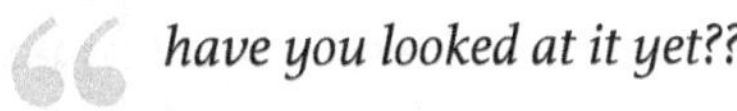

AFTER PUTTING THE PHONE DOWN, I sighed. I wanted to return to editing my post but I knew it would cause me to forget about the message entirely. My brain was good at forgetting to respond to conversations I didn't want to have.

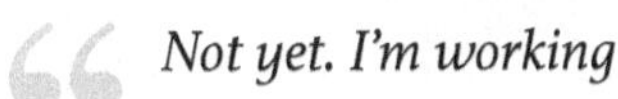

I LOCKED my phone and put it face down on the table to return to my blog. I had just begun to regain focus when I heard the buzzing of my phone again. *Dear Lord,* I thought. It couldn't have been more than a minute.

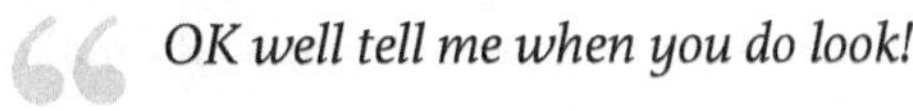

Another sigh escaped as I set my phone down. I could almost see her eager face through the screen. It was the same youthful expression I always attached to Rosie when she was excited.

I glanced back to the blog post sitting like an unfinished painting on the screen in front of me. It was going to be good, but it needed a little more work. The editing process was crucial. As much as I hated editing, it was when I could polish the piece and ensure it had the real edge that my readers wanted.

Without thinking, I stole another look at my phone. Her quick response was evidence that she was sitting in anticipation and it was almost as if she was sitting in the room with me, bouncing on her feet and distracting me. *Oh Rosie*, I muttered to myself. She had officially succeeded in stealing my attention away from my work. *I guess I could use a break*, I thought.

I picked up my phone and typed a quick response.

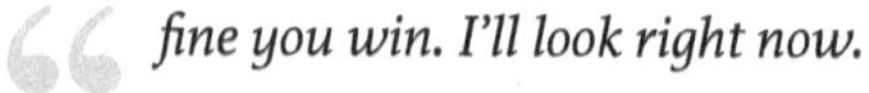

fine you win. I'll look right now.

I imagined Rosie's smiling face as I sent the message and felt relief in knowing that at least I was making someone happy. I scanned the desk for the post-it note I had used to write down the log in info. For a second I caught myself wishing it had gotten lost—as if that somehow would magically make the profile vanish along with it—but I quickly found it beneath a scratch piece of paper.

It all felt odd, like I was a detective of some sort, as I logged in and opened my profile. It was familiar and yet different enough to be almost creepy. Everything was about me, but I hadn't done any of it. Even my picture at the top of the screen looked like a different person smiling back at me. *I need to change this picture if I want this profile to go anywhere,* I thought to myself. I looked far to innocent and happy to be on a dating site. Below the picture was a small space for a bio with a few short sentences Rosie had already written.

> *I'm Harper! I'm smart and single living in Miami and enjoying that warm Florida sun. I love writing and football. (Go Bluejays!) I'm also a big fan of long walks on the beach and getting caught in the rain.*

IMMEDIATELY THE PASSAGE IRKED ME. I would never use something as trite as "getting caught in the rain" on a profile. I reread the sentences a few more times, each time leaving more of a sour taste in my mouth. This was going to be a disaster.

Her description wasn't *wrong,* at least not factually. And it probably wasn't all that out of place for the Internet, but it was drastically different than anything I would have written. I would have *never* described myself this way in a million years. The passage was way too happy and optimistic. It read like the bio of a young high school girl and it sounded... *preppy?* How in the world had they derived a preppy sounding bio with me in mind?

I almost gave up on the website right then and there, but the format of the bio made me worried that there was more toxic information below that I needed to be aware of. Had my sister not thought that, while she was carelessly building this profile, she was also introducing the world to a personality that I couldn't take back?

With a scowl I continued to scroll down the page. The design and infrastructure of the website was actually quite charming. The page had a warm color scheme and an aesthetically pleasing make-up. There were several boxes to respond to questions on hobbies, education and other various talking points. It was light years ahead of my other dating websites. It was easy to see the difference between paid and free.

I continued to read through the answers my sister had come up with. Her responses were filled with an overwhelming optimism and sense of vigor that seemed to scream up at you from the page. It was all sunshine and joy, with only glimpses of my usual sarcasm, but even that had a happy slant to it.

There was something gnawing in the back of my mind that caused me to stop and pause for an instant. *Is this really how my sister sees me?* I wondered. Is this really how she thinks *I* would have answered? She had sought Thomas's help in building the profile... is this how *he* thinks of me? I could hear Rosie's words echoing in my head, *he actually does a really good impression of you.* Did my sister and my brother-in-law really see me as a walking bundle of blissful joy?

I guess it's not the worst image they could have painted, I thought. *But is this really how I come off to them?* What had I done to leave that impression? And more, what had I done to give them the impression that this is how I would describe *myself*?

My mother, on the other hand, would have certainly come up with answers far different than these. *I wonder whose work would have been more dangerous,* I thought with a chuckle. My mother probably would have posted that I wanted a family right away and that I wanted as many kids as possible.

Finally, I clicked on a tab on the bottom right corner of the screen that said, *"Chat."* A screen unfolded with numerous conversation bubbles. At the top of the screen was the name, "Gabe."

Gabe. I repeated it out loud. Names are always important. They carry the tone of the person and are part of the first impression. A Nichole gives a very different vibe than a Nicki.

This one wasn't bad. It actually had kind of a strong, masculine tone yet it wasn't too stiff. I actually liked his name. *It's too bad I'll have to change it when it comes time for your blog post,* I thought and laughed to myself.

I scrolled to the top of the conversation. Rosie and Thomas had apparently rather enjoyed conversing through my mask. There must have been fifteen, twenty, maybe even thirty messages between them and this so called 'Gabe.'

A groan escaped from my throat as I glanced at the clock above my desk. It was already close to midnight. I looked back to the computer and conversation in front of me. It was like a book that I was only just beginning. *I'm too tired for this,* I thought. *And I don't have the energy.* Meeting Optimistic Happy Harper had taken it out of me. And I didn't want to begin a book that I knew I couldn't finish before passing out. *I'll come back when I'm able to read through the whole thing in one sitting,* I told myself.

I felt another small surge of relief. I had avoided the full reality for at least one more night. Part of me still felt like a nosey detective snooping around someone else's personal business. At least I wasn't the one who had intrusively made the account in the first place. *And* signed someone else up for a date!

I thought about closing my computer and heading to bed, but I was still curious about this guy. *If I am going to go through with this date then I should at least do my homework,* I thought and clicked on his name at the top of the screen.

His picture was the headshot Rosie had showed me initially and I began clicking through his other pictures. They were all candid shots with him looking happy and pleasant. He wore a smile that was gentle and rose into his cheeks. In most pictures, his hair maintained its slightly messy ruffle, but in every picture his green eyes sparkled. They seemed almost brighter than the screen. He was definitely in good shape and he looked to be slightly taller than average standing next to his friends.

I scrolled to his bio.

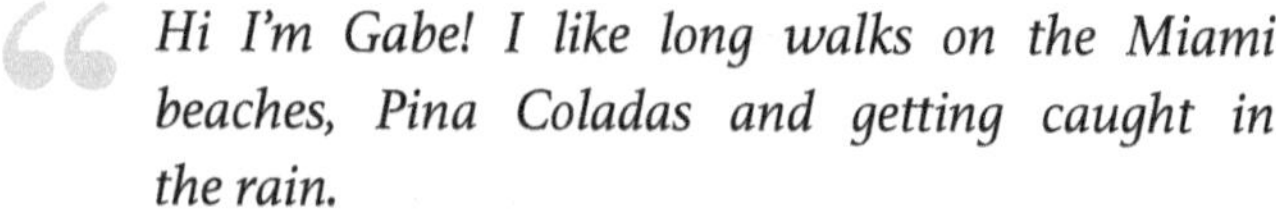

> *Hi I'm Gabe! I like long walks on the Miami beaches, Pina Coladas and getting caught in the rain.*

MY TEMPLES TENSED SUBCONSCIOUSLY at first and then with an irritated squint. No wonder he had picked my bio- we were practically twins. *Does he really think this works,* I thought. *Attractive guys can be so naïve. This bio is going to work well in his future blog post.* I had almost stopped reading at the end of the sentence but something drew my eyes to the rest of his bio.

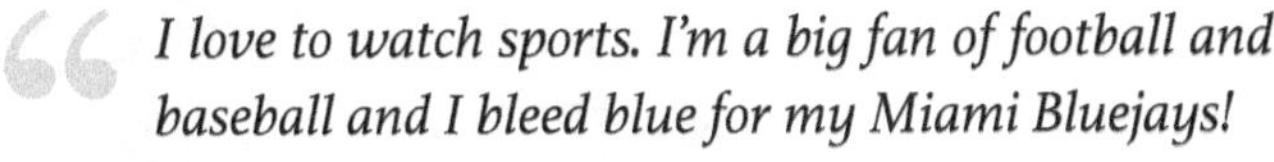

> *I love to watch sports. I'm a big fan of football and baseball and I bleed blue for my Miami Bluejays!*

A SHORT SPOUT of elation shot up from my stomach and into my chest. Sports fan. Bluejays fan.

At least that meant we would have *something* to talk about on the date. I had been on a few quiet dates and they were always awful to write about. Not that they ever went well, but silently and awkwardly looking down at your plate the whole time doesn't exactly make for riveting blog material, even when the guy is a total train wreck—as they almost always were.

I sent Rosie a mental high-five. Ever since we were kids, Rosie had always known about my intense love for sports. She often joked that if football were a guy I would have married him long before ever getting a chance to start my blog. Clearly, she had remembered this passion when writing my bio. And evidently he liked sports enough to put it in his bio. *That's probably the whole reason we matched in the first place. Stupid, bogus algorithms that matched us off the keywords in our bios. How brilliant,* I thought.

Well it was settled, I would have to talk about sports the whole time. But I could do that. I could talk about sports all day. *If this guy knows what he's talking about this might actually be kind of fun,* I thought and then stopped. I paused and stared blankly at my computer as the mouse hovered on the screen. *Fun? Did that thought really just cross my mind? When was the last time a date was actually fun?* It had been awhile. So long that I couldn't really even remember what a *fun* date felt like.

I blinked away the daydream and blew the hair out of my face. *What am I thinking? This date will be like all the others. Why would it be any different?*

After another hurried glance at the clock, I closed the webpage and sank in my chair. That was enough for the night. The clock read past midnight and I needed to finish editing my blog so it could be posted. I would do more research on this guy later, for there was more research to be done. Inside everyone was the potential for a catastrophic date.

I knew this guy, with his dark windblown hair and sparkling green eyes, was no exception. There was the potential for a good blog post somewhere inside of him. The only problem was that he was good at shielding his signs of disaster. He had already successfully hidden them from Rosie. But all it would take was discovering his particular brand of crazy.

CHAPTER 4

"So, what do you think, Cora?" Anticipation bubbled through my voice.

"So good!" she paused, obviously re-reading a section. "I think it's your best one yet to be honest!"

I let out a grateful sigh. If my best friend Cora said a blog post was good, it was golden. She was the most honest and appreciated critic of my work.

I had finished and posted my blog late last night and had woken to a barrage of comments. My readers were the reason I loved my work. It was always nice to wake up to great feedback after a long night. Their comments made all the bad dates worth it.

"This is more hits than you've gotten in awhile, yeah?" she asked. I could hear her clicking around on her computer over the phone.

"Yeah, I think so" I said, scrolling down the comments. I was glad to see such a positive response to the post. Cora was right, there were more comments and shares than I had received in awhile.

"I guess Bathroom Dude was a big hit! Wait, hold on,"

she said as there was a muffling noise from the other end of the phone. I could hear scratching as Cora moved the phone from her face and then bits and pieces from her side conversation.

"Okay, I'm back," she said again.

"Really, Cora? You're having a double shot at dinner?" I asked while also slightly covering a laugh.

"Hey don't eavesdrop! And it's fine, that stuff barely touches me anyway."

"You're insane," I said as I reached for the post-it note with my login information.

"Me? You're the one going out on a date your sister set you up on. Where are you going again?" she asked.

"Dinner. Keepin' it simple," I said. I opened up the Kindling Dating website and began browsing. My humiliating profile, the chat conversation and the website as a whole seemed much less intimidating now after the success of my last post. Success had an odd medicinal effect. I was too excited about my good post to be anxious about the Kindling Dating website or my upcoming date.

Cora chuckled. "I think it's awesome. Tell Rosie she has my complete respect."

"You tell her," I scoffed.

"Oh, I totally will next time I'm in town," Cora promised.

"Does that mean you're coming to town?" I asked hopefully. My tone was equipped with a persuasive attempt in it. Cora lived in Orlando, and although we were in the same state it still required a three and a half hour drive either way, which made coordinating visits rather difficult. I needed to see my best friend much more than I actually got to.

"Not any time soon. Sorry, girl," she said. "Work has been crazy. I've been picking up extra shifts left and right until we can hire somebody new. It sucks."

"Darn. I was hoping," I said solemnly.

"Yeah, I know. Me too," she said. "Now quit changing the subject! I want to know more about this date! Tell me everything."

I gave an obnoxious sigh into the phone before I began, "Well, his name is Gabe. He's a business owner."

"Nice!" she interrupted. "Maybe that means he'll pay for dinner this time!"

I laughed and started filling out a date request on the website. "A girl can dream."

"What are you doing?" she asked starkly, "I keep hearing your keys typing. Are you writing another blog or something?"

"No," I hesitated for an instant, my fingers hovering guiltily over the keys. "I'm actually signing up for another date..."

"Really? Already?" she asked, impressed. "You haven't even met this guy yet."

"Yeah I know, I'm..." I began, but trailed off as I looked for the submit button.

"You think things are going to go that well?"

"No, I mean with another guy," I replied, frowning. Why in the world would I set up a second date with a guy I hadn't even met yet?

"What? Why?" she was genuinely surprised. "This guy sounds like the most promising guy not for your blog that you've had in a long time."

"Because, Cora. I'm hedging my bets," I explained.

"Hedging your bets?" she asked. I could hear the displeased expression on her face. She was almost as bad as Rosie.

"Yeah, I need bad dates to fuel my blog. Did you forget that that's how I pay my bills?"

Cora sighed. "Yeah, I get that Harper," she said. "But don't you feel like you should at least give him a chance?"

"I am giving him a chance! We have a date scheduled, don't we?"

"Well yeah, but you're already assuming it's going to go badly." She sounded disappointed.

"I have experience with these things, Cora," I said. If I wasn't sitting at my computer, I would have put my hands on my hips.

"I think it's just wishful thinking for your blog. And I don't know if that's healthy…"

I rolled my eyes. "You sound like my sister right now."

"Well, maybe we both just want you to find someone you actually like," she said. "You deserve some love in your life."

"Actually, you sound like my mom," I decided. "And that's much worse."

"Please," she said, and I could hear her put her glass down. "Just give this guy a chance? I have a good feeling about this one."

I allowed silence to be my response. All of the women in my life were hoping this would be my Prince Charming and I was the only one sane enough to be cautious. I was just glad I wasn't talking to my Mom, Rosie, and Cora all at the same time. Those were the ingredients for a storm that could wipe out the whole Florida coast.

"What if he's the perfect guy for you, Harper?" Cora asked after a moment.

I laughed silently to myself. "Cora there is no such thing as a perfect guy," I said.

After repeating this same conversation with different people I had developed an inventory of preset responses. Why everyone was so certain that this was a 'perfect match' was beyond me. "Like I said, putting another date or two in the books is just hedging my bets. If he is the *perfect guy,* then I can just cancel them."

"I don't know, Harper..." Cora trailed off as she spoke.

"And besides, everyone knows *you're* my soulmate!" I said with a sort of exaggerated flare.

Cora laughed. "Okay. I *am* your soul mate," she agreed. "I have to get some work done. I want to know all the details about the date! And the guy. I want to know everything."

"Of course!"

"Alright. I'll talk to you soon. Love you," she carried the last syllable affectionately.

"Love you too, Cora," I said and hung up.

I set my phone down on my desk and continued scrolling through my old dating profile on the free website. I wasn't quite ready to test the waters with a second date from the same expensive site. What if the dating algorithm Kindling Dating actually worked? Besides, I didn't want to go through and have to change all of Rosie's hard work.

No, I knew that if I wanted a bad date, I should go with my tried and true method. Free dating site with answers that were actually applicable. If I wanted to meet actual guys, I needed to come up with better answers. Rosie's answers on Kindling Dating were mostly true, but so off the mark as to what men wanted. I had to put what guys were looking for. Not what I actually was.

I clicked to the page with my next top match on my old dating site and began scanning his profile before confirming the date. He looked nice enough. A Miami man named Dave who liked deep-sea fishing and bowling. There was nothing on his profile that screamed *warning,* but then again, there usually never was. At least not with the sane ones. I had seen enough profiles in my life to know that they're never exactly as advertised. Even if their personalities were riddled with trouble, most men were at least competent enough to know what to reveal and what not to reveal on a dating profile. This profile was no different. He knew how to disguise his brand of crazy, whatever it was.

The problem was that Rosie and Cora hadn't seen the hundreds of online dating profiles that I had. I'd seen them all—good and bad—and I knew how they played out. If they consistently saw all the pitiful profiles that I did, they would share the same pessimism. They would understand that the best and most likely scenario would mean more material for my blog. And this one—I continued scrolling through his profile and descriptions—looked like it would make perfect blog fodder.

I clicked the button to send the confirmation. Now I just had to wait for him to reply. I felt like delving into more matches to find more potential blog suitors, but I remembered my conversation with Cora. *Maybe she's right, maybe it's not the healthiest approach,* I thought. But regardless, the success of my recent post was evidence that I was doing *something* right.

Instead of looking for more matches, I clicked back to Kindling Dating and to the match that Rosie had found. Gabe.

The smile in his picture sure was charming. It was like he was beaming up at me through the computer screen. His smile was piercing and his emerald eyes locked on me as if he were standing two feet away and making eye contact. I felt the urge to smile back.

I knew that it was dangerous to get too smitten with someone's online profile picture. Lots of people hide behind a good photo, but evidently there was some reason that Kindling Dating thought that we would make a good match. A perfect match, if that was even possible.

Were their algorithms really capable of assembling the perfect fit? The whole concept of a 'perfect fit' in general had always seemed cliché to me. Certainly great fits and happy couples existed. I had seen proof of happy marriages between two people that worked great for each other. But they were never between two people as... particular... as myself. They were always between two nice and pleasant people, not a pair of sarcastic realists, whose best friends also happened to be extremely sarcastic.

For a second I paused and chuckled at the idea of marrying Cora. There's no doubt it would be intensely amusing, but we would drive each other up the wall.

Although isn't that the whole idea of marriage, I thought. *Find someone that you enjoy enough not to kill when they drive you insane?*

I caught myself staring off into space, imagining what a perfect marriage would look like, and I made an effort to refocus. There was research that needed to be done.

I started writing my message to Mr. Bowler.

CHAPTER 5

The computer screen glowed against the backdrop of the oncoming evening. The dark blue of the sky as night fell was soft and comforting like a blanket around a child. It was another warm night in Miami and the intense heat of the day had mellowed into a pleasant temperature and the humidity was actually comfortable. On a normal night, my computer screen became the only light in the room and I used it to get lost in my blog.

However, this evening was different. On this particular evening I needed to research and make sure I was prepared for my date. I had gone deep into the conversation that my sister had begun. I was like a student studying over a text-book before a big test; I knew their conversation held valu-able information, it was a matter of trying to dissect it and uncover his personality.

The mask that Rosie had assumed while trying to imitate me was hilarious. I had already scanned their conversation several times and had paused frequently to laugh out loud. She either had no idea how to flirt with someone online, or she was too concerned with compensating for my personality that she just sounded absurd. Or more likely, a brutal combination of both.

I wondered if he had also thought she sounded absurd. He seemed to have been receptive though, and we were going on a date, so apparently it wasn't too awful. I kept going back through to re-read various portions of their exchange to make sure I wasn't going to say anything contradictory.

- He had initiated the conversation: **Hey whats up? I saw your picture and thought you were cute.**
- Rosie had replied: **Hey! You're not too bad lookin yourself.**
- Gabe: **I usually hover around a 7 on a good day.**
- Rosie: **I guess your picture was taken on an extra good day then.**
- Gabe: **Why? You think I'm looking more like a 7 ½?**
- Rosie: **Maybe even a 7 and ¾ ...**

I COULDN'T HELP but laugh again. It wasn't awful but the idea of Rosie flirting like that while her husband looked on was hysterical. She had made an obvious attempt to sound flirty, which worked better on some occasions than others, but overall it wasn't a terrible effort. It was still weird to imagine Rosie trying so hard to sound like me. Most of their messages were amusing but they were also far from what I would have said. There was still a little too much Rosie seeping through, no matter how hard she had tried to mask it. *I sure hope he doesn't expect me to be this sweet in person,* I thought.

- At one point he had said; **So is this how you usually spend your Saturday nights?**
- And Rosie had replied with; **Idk... I like to switch it up and keep it interesting...**

I WANTED to slap my sister through the screen. *Is that really how she thinks I would have responded to that? It's a wonder this guy still wants to go on a date with me,* I thought.

The conversation got a little better after the topic of sports was introduced and I was immediately glad to see he had brought it up.

- Gabe: **So you're a Bluejays fan huh?**
- Rosie: **I'm the biggest Bluejays fan there is!**
- *Again, not how I would have phrased that, but okay sis.*
- He wrote back; **I'd be willing to make a bet on that one. No way you're a bigger fan than me.**

ROSIE REPLIED with more frivolous banter. She had refrained from interjecting any sort of real sports talk, and I was glad. Knowing Rosie, she would have attempted to sound clever and like she knew what she was talking about, but anyone with an actual understanding of football would have seen right through it. I wondered if Thomas had stepped in and told her to hold back. *Most likely,* I decided.

The topic of sports trailed off probably after he realized it wasn't really going anywhere. In person I would have to revive his faith in me as a sports fan, but that was okay. He had transitioned by asking about my work.

- He wrote; **Ha ha I guess we'll see. So what do you do for work then?**
- Rosie wrote back; **I'm a writer! What about you?**
- Gabe: **Oh that's cool! What do you write about? I kind of do some writing for work, too.**
- Rosie: **No way! I write articles, what kind of stuff do you write about?**
- Gabe: **Wow that's really cool. I'm not actually that much of a writer I guess. I just write code- ha. I own my own business.**

Yeah, writing code isn't quite the same, buddy, I thought and chuckled to myself. Rosie replied with a joke about writing code that I figured had probably come from Thomas. He then jabbed back by asking whether I wrote articles for *The Wall Street Journal* or for *Playboy Magazine.* I laughed again. *Not bad dude. But if only you knew,* I thought. Luckily Rosie hadn't disclosed any specifics about my blog.

The conversation continued with more playful mockery and teasing. He seemed like a decent enough guy. He was a little bro-y, but that was okay, I could be a bit of a bro myself. Besides that he was funny and even a little clever. He sounded smart and for a second I found myself slightly interested by his persona. He had managed to lead a pretty fun and entertaining conversation, despite having to deal with Rosie's uncanny sort of demeanor.

I found myself fixating on certain messages where he seemed particularly crafty. He sounded like a fun person to talk to and I wondered if he would maintain the same sense of clever confidence in person that he had shown online. The ones with strong online personalities and a weak physical presence were the worst. Then again, whatever personality he had put forth online was immediately more than any effort of mine. Any idea he had of my personality was fabricated. In all my days of writing a dating blog, I had never imagined I would be following a blueprint laid down by my sister.

My phone beeped loudly, startling me and reminding me that it was time to get ready. I took a deep breath and stood from my computer.

It was time to see how accurate this *perfect match* really was. Time to see if he was really as charming as he seemed online. I wasn't usually the type that attracted gentlemen, but maybe Rosie was. After all, she had landed Thomas and he was a good guy. I could see myself being happy with a guy like Thomas. Evidently, she had done enough to make this guy interested in me, or interested enough to *consider* being interested in me. It was time to find out.

Trying to match an expectation set by my sister was going to be weird. Whatever blueprint she had laid had been with me in mind, but still, their conversation was littered with things I would never say. It was all based on things Rosie thought I would say. Whether or not he liked or disliked those things, they weren't going to be what showed up on our date tonight. I wasn't going to fake a personality, even if it was supposed to be me in the first place.

Though I wondered how many times had I encountered someone with a million different faces. People who appeared to be one thing online, only to be completely different in real life. *Too many to count,* I thought. My readers would have known the answer to that.

Perhaps there had even been times when I had come across differently online than in person. Even though I tried to come across as real as possible, it was a natural problem with online dating and a certain level of variance could always be expected.

Even if Mr. Perfect Match had fallen in love with the character Rosie had created, he was going to get *me*. He was going to meet the girl that my sister had attempted to imitate. And if I couldn't live up to her imitation and his fantasy, then that would be on him. He would have to learn that *perfect matches* aren't the same in the real world as they are online.

I had already showered and was finishing the final touches of my make-up. It was kind of funny how my mind had wandered, I thought. I had spent the entire preparation process worrying about trying to live up to an online profile that I hadn't even created. I was nervous about being the bad date instead of having one and I laughed. *That's new,* I thought. *I guess if you write about bad dates long enough you start to become one.*

I buckled my shoes around my ankle. We had planned a dinner with a walk and I had selected a decent pair of black wedges without much of a heel that would be comfortable and sexy. The restaurant was slightly fancy, but I had been on enough dates that I no longer stressed over my outfit. I wore my favorite dark blue dress. It was just the right amount of classy without going overboard.

Dinner and a walk had been his idea and Rosie had

happily agreed. He had also recommended the restaurant. At the very least a nice dinner would be enjoyable, as long as I wasn't conned into paying extravagantly again. The walk would be something new. I wondered where he was planning on taking me, or if we were just going to walk around the restaurant. Either could be interesting.

A walk also means that I'll have a lot of open space to run if things get really bad, I thought and almost laughed again as gathered my purse and stepped out the door.

Okay, Mr. Perfect Match. I'm ready for my date.

CHAPTER 6

Here comes another great blog post, I thought, as I stood outside of the very nice restaurant and reevaluated my shoe choice. I frowned and hear Rosie's voice in my head. *No, be nice. It might be great.*

Given my dating history, I wasn't expecting much. The best I could really hope for was that I wouldn't get stuck with the bill like last time. If that happened at this restaurant, I'd have to go to the poor house. *Dove's* was one of the nicest places in town and a two-person meal would be the same amount as a quarter of my rent.

A well-dressed hostess greeted me as I entered. I was fairly sure that she made more as a waitress here than I did as a blogger.

"I'm meeting someone, but I'm not sure if he's here yet," I explained, as I took off my sunglasses and put them in my purse. "I can just wait at the bar."

"Of course," the woman said, as she turned and led me across the restaurant to a beautiful bar next to a giant window overlooking the ocean. "Enjoy your dinner."

She pulled the chair out for me and I sat down. I

checked my watch. We were at go time. If this guy was late like the other one, I wasn't going to stick around.

Five minutes, that's all this guy gets before I'm leaving, I promised myself.

"Good evening, ma'am. My name is Alandro." A charming bartender grinned over the bar at me. "Can I start you off with something to drink?"

I'll bet they charge for water here, I thought, glancing at the very expensive drink menu. *Water with ice must cost even more.*

"I think I'm okay for now," I said. "I'm meeting someone and I'd rather just order when they get here."

The waiter's eyes lit up as he pointed across the restaurant. "Is that the man you're meeting? He mentioned that he was meeting a pretty girl tonight and I assume he must have been talking about you."

I smiled at the compliment and looked in the direction that the waiter was pointing. A handsome man in a black suit sat by himself at a table in the opposite corner. My jaw practically hit the floor when I saw him. He looked exactly like he did in the pictures on his dating profile, something that I was not accustomed to seeing.

"You know, that actually *is* the person I'm meeting," I responded, as I stood up and followed the waiter to the other table. "Thank you."

The man with dark hair and green eyes looked up from a menu as I approached. He looked familiar for some reason, and it wasn't just because I had seen his photos on his dating profile. It felt like I had seen him other places too, but I just couldn't quite put my finger on when or where.

Oh well, not important, I thought. *I've met so many people with my dating blog. They all start looking familiar after awhile.*

His lips curled up into a smile as he set the menu on the table in front of him and stood up. "Harper?"

"Gabe?"

We shook hands and then he stepped around me and pulled out my chair like a true gentleman.

Wow. I can't remember the last time a guy did that, I thought. It was actually really charming. Point to Mr. Perfect Match.

"It's really good to meet you," he said, as he walked back to his chair and sat down.

"Good to meet you, too." I responded with a smile.

The guy was gorgeous, so at least no matter how the evening went, I'd have something nice to look at. Given my previous hundred dates, though, my hopes were still about as low as possible.

"What can I bring you to drink?" a waiter asked, coming up to the table.

"Um, I'll just take a water," I said, flashing another smile. For some reason, I was nervous. I never felt nervous on dates, but this one was different.

"That's all you want?" Gabe asked. He smiled and motioned to the menu. "You can order whatever you like."

That's what the last guy said and then I ended up paying for it. I shook my head and smiled. "Just water," I repeated. "Thank you, though."

Gabe shrugged. "I'll take a dirty martini," he told the waiter.

"Sounds great, sir," replied the waiter. "I'll be back with your drinks."

The waiter scurried away and I shifted in my seat. The initial awkwardness of a first meeting was definitely in the air, and even though I had been on tons dates, I still couldn't shake it. Luckily, Gabe didn't let the silence last very long.

"So, Harper, tell me about yourself," he said, leaning back in his chair but keeping those green eyes focused on me.

"There's not a whole lot to tell," I responded. "I work as a writer for a magazine. What about you?"

"I remember you said something about that." He smiled and leaned forward. His dark hair fell across his brow, somehow making him even more attractive. "What do you write? Anything I'd recognize?"

He seemed genuinely interested, which actually made me a little nervous. Very few of my dates ever seemed this interested. I obviously couldn't tell him about the blog I ran, since I knew later that night I'd be writing about this date and the last thing I wanted was him looking me up.

"Oh, nothing special. Just articles here and there. A little of this, a little of that. I'm freelance, so I don't work for a specific magazine." I shrugged, trying to play it cool and tell him enough without actively lying. "I just take the work as it comes. Sometimes I write about the latest marathon in town and other times I'll write about football."

"I love football," he said, with a smile. "It's my guilty pleasure."

"Mine too," I said, feeling some of my nerves fade. "Sundays are the only times that nobody can get ahold of me. My whole family knows that I won't answer my phone if a game is on."

Gabe laughed and leaned back in his chair. His laugh was easy and confident. It made me want to join in.

"I wouldn't have taken you for a football fan," he said. "No offense, but you're kind of missing the beer gut and sideburns."

"Come on now, not every football fan is like that," I said

with a laugh. "Besides, I'm working on my sideburns. I think they're coming in quite nicely, actually."

Any initial awkwardness was quickly vanishing. It was unusual for a first date, but nothing to write home about. Some men were just good at talking to people and I assumed that's all it was. I started taking mental notes so that when I wrote the blog a little later, I'd have all the details I'd need to make an interesting post.

"What do you do, Gabe?" I asked.

"I am a..." he started to say, pausing as the waiter came up and delivered our drinks.

Here we go, I thought. *This is where he fluffs up his position at whatever company he works for. This is where he tells me he's a "Master of the Custodial Arts" when in reality he's just a janitor.*

"Software engineer for my own business," he finished. He took a sip of his martini and smiled.

"So what does that entail?" I asked, hoping he'd give me something juicy to write about later. "What kind of software?"

"Oh nothing special really. A little of this, a little of that. I just take the work as it comes," he said with a sly smile.

"Is that right?" I played with the straw in my water, swirling the ice around as I smiled. He was poking fun at me for my vague response to his similar question, but I actually liked it. This guy had a backbone and he wasn't letting me walk all over him.

"Yeah, it's just a job," he responded with a shrug that made me notice just how broad his shoulders were. "Kind of boring, honestly. Unless you like typing and looking at numbers all day. It's not exactly riveting date conversation."

"But you own your own business?" I asked, trying to remember exactly what his profile had said.

"Well, me and two other guys own the company," he

explained. "I run all the computer code and software programming for it."

"You don't exactly look like the 'computer nerd' type," I said. I motioned to his perfect hair, smoking body, and confident smile.

"What, do you think we all look the same?" he responded. "I left my pocket protector and nerd glasses at home just for this date. I can run back and get them if you want."

"How else am I supposed to believe you work on computers for a living?" I asked, laughing. "I brought a pen and paper just to prove I'm a writer."

Gabe chuckled as he grabbed his martini and held it in the air.

"Let's cheers. How about to new people in our lives?" he asked.

"To *potential* new people in our lives," I corrected him. I wasn't quite ready to mark this date in the win category just yet. We still had a full meal to go and anything could happen, but for the first time in a long time, it looked actually possible.

We clinked our glasses and I took a sip of my water. Gabe was seriously charming, witty and beyond gorgeous. I feared that I was actually kind of enjoying myself, which was very strange for me. We chatted lightly about things, like where we grew up and how we fell into our lines of work. He was so easy to talk to that I found myself forgetting that we were on a date.

"What would you like to eat?" he asked, as the waiter approached us.

I hadn't even looked at the menu. I had been too into our conversation.

"Um, I'll just take an appetizer," I said, glancing at the

menu. I picked the cheapest thing I could find. "Maybe grilled asparagus or something."

"Harper, order whatever you like," Gabe urged, though he didn't specifically say that he'd be picking up the tab.

"I'd rather have something light, though. I'm not super hungry." I flashed him a grin. It wasn't a lie: butterflies had begun to flow inside of me, which had put my appetite in check.

What is this guy doing to me? I wondered. I was pretty sure that my blog had killed all the first date jitters, but apparently not.

I stuck with the grilled asparagus appetizer and Gabe got a 10-ounce filet mignon. The waiter took our orders and disappeared around the corner. Gabe sipped his martini before fixing me with his piercing green eyes. It was impossible to not feel like the center of the universe when he looked at me like that.

"I have to know, what's your favorite football team?" Gabe asked.

"The Miami Blue Jays, of course," I said, as my eyes grew wide. I could have sworn we had already "chatted" about this. Or rather, he and Rosie had. Maybe he had just forgotten or was making conversation. "They're the best team in the nation."

"The best in the nation?" Gabe looked thoughtful. "I mean they're good. Really good. But they haven't been to the playoffs in six years."

"So what? I don't care if they never go to the playoffs again, they're still the best team because they're from the town I live in," I shot back. "I'm no bandwagon fan. Blue Jays all the way, rain or shine, I'll still cheer them on. They're *my* team."

Gabe's eyes were locked with mine and I found myself

falling into them. His green irises looked like something out of a painting, too beautiful to be real. They were emerald green, like the rolling hills of Ireland, but more exotic.

"I'm actually glad you said that," he said, a smile splitting his face in two. "The Blue Jays are my team also. I just wanted to make sure we didn't love rival teams or something."

"Yeah, that wouldn't have worked out," I joked. "I couldn't date a Crows fan. The fights when they lost would just be too hard."

Gabe leaned his head back and laughed. "I agree completely."

We nibbled on our food while we talked and for the first time on any date ever, I found myself not wanting it to end. The food was delicious, but I was actually more interested in Gabe than the meal. By the time dessert came, I had all but forgotten that the reason I even went on the date was so that I'd have more material for another blog post. In fact, my website and blog were the last thing on my mind. I was actually *into* this guy and interested in what he had to say. I couldn't believe it.

"Dessert?" he asked. "The tiramisu is amazing here."

I nodded. "That's actually one of my favorite desserts."

Am I on Candid Camera or something? I asked myself. A part of me thought my sister was going to pop out from behind a nearby booth any second and tell me that the whole thing was a set up, and that Gabe was a friend of hers who she'd paid to play some elaborate prank on me. This scenario seemed more likely than a date going right for once.

I hated the fact that I felt suspicious of any guy that didn't totally offend me or make me feel awkward, but I couldn't help it. He was just so different than the other men. I didn't know what to do with myself.

How am I supposed to deal with a date that's gone well? And why is it so horrifying to me? I wondered. *I should be able to handle this!*

Gabe ordered us a tiramisu to share, which we took turns eating as we conversed.

"So have you met a lot of good people on Kindling Dating?" he asked, taking a bite of dessert.

I nearly spit out my mouthful in response. Maybe he did know who I was and this was an elaborate joke.

"This is actually my first date using Kindling," I replied cautiously.

His eyes widened at my response. "Really? You seem really good at first dates for this to be your first one."

"Oh, it's just my first time with Kindling," I said. "I've used other dating sites."

"How's this one stacking up compared to those?" he asked. I wasn't sure, but he seemed nervous about my answer. It was actually kind of adorable.

Play it cool, Harper. Play it cool, I thought. This date was a thousand times better, maybe even a million times better than my usual ones. I was actually attracted to this guy and the conversation was so smooth and easy. If I wasn't in the business of bad dates, I would give Kindling Dating an A+ at this point.

I couldn't actually say any of that, though.

"Yeah, this date seems to be going pretty well," I responded, trying to act nonchalant about it. I was pretty sure he could see right through me.

"Good," he said, another one of his amazing smiles crossing his face. "I'm glad. And I agree. It's going pretty well. I've been having a lot of fun getting to know you. A lot of fun."

I hung onto his words like they were the greatest thing ever said. His voice was deep and sexy. He oozed a relaxed confidence that made me squirm in my seat. I felt like it wouldn't have taken much for him to get me out of my dress.

The waiter approached and asked, "Can I get you two anything else this evening?"

"I'm stuffed," I responded, as I patted my belly. It wasn't really true, but there was no way I was ordering more. Not when I knew how much my asparagus had cost.

"I think we're good," Gabe told the waiter.

I watched as the bill was pulled out from behind the waiter's back. It was like slow motion as he set it on the table in front of us.

Who's going to pick it up? I pray that he doesn't stick me with the whole thing.

"Should we split it?" I asked, without any hesitation. It was why I had ordered the cheapest thing I could find on the menu.

Gabe looked at me like I was crazy as he reached forward and grabbed the bill, pulling it toward his side of the table.

"That's a very nice offer, but I'll get it," he said, reaching for his wallet.

Okay, now I know for sure that this guy isn't real, I thought. *Charming, sweet, and pays for dinner? What kind of weird date was I on?*

"Are you positive? I can pay for my half," I said. I meant it. Mostly.

"No way," Gabe responded. "This was my choice of restaurant and our first date. There's not a chance I'm letting you pay for this. It's my treat."

Both my mind and my pocketbook felt deep relief from his words. Gabe paid for the bill with cash and then scooted his chair back.

"Well, would you like to get out of here?" he asked. "I did promise a walk."

"Sure," I said.

Normally, this would have been the time when I'd have jumped in my car and driven home immediately to write the latest blog post. But I had nothing to write about. This date had gone exceptionally well. Too well, to be honest. I had no idea what I would write about this one.

Deep breaths, Harper. Just don't trip over these heels or scratch your ass through this dress and you'll be fine. Just relax and smile and keep flirting. This evening could get interesting if you let it.

CHAPTER 7

I stood up from the table and followed Gabe out of the restaurant.

It had been so long since I'd even had the slightest inclination to let a date go farther. The thought actually terrified me. The butterflies in my stomach started mambo-ing.

Gabe tipped the hostess as we walked through the doors and into the street. The sun dipped behind the ocean and was replaced with the fluorescent lights of the street lamps.

Dove's was located along the beach in a commercial area. There was a short path to the water that would give us a nice stroll. It wasn't a long walk, but it would be a nice way to end the evening.

The water rippled under the moonlight. For a moment I thought I saw a flash of a dolphin in the waves, but I was fairly sure it was just my over-excited imagination. There was no way I was lucky enough to have a good date and see dolphins. We had the path to ourselves, although we were clearly visible to everyone in the restaurant.

"Have you ever been to a Blue Jays game?" Gabe asked. It wasn't the question I was expecting.

"Uh, I sat in the cheap seats once," I replied, feeling a little off balance. "It was amazing getting to see the team live, even if I needed binoculars to see them. What about you?"

"A couple of games," he answered. "I try and go as often as I can."

"As often as you can?" I asked, pausing as we approached the water. The ocean was absolutely beautiful. I could see the lights of several boats out on the water and the tropical air was cool as it came off the water. "How many do you get to go to?"

"I may have season tickets," he admitted slowly. He turned to face me, a small smile lit up by the moon on the waves. "But don't let that change how you view me."

"Season tickets?" I squeaked. "Can I marry you?"

He laughed. "I told you not to let that change your opinion of me."

I grinned. "It doesn't. In fact, it just makes me like you more."

I immediately felt my face flush. This wasn't like me on a first date. He was making me nervous and excited all at the same time. I didn't want this moment to end and at the same time, it was a form of torture to not be in complete control of the date. I wanted more, yet was terrified of what could happen next.

He smiled back and took a deep breath. We were at the end of the path. There was no where else for us to go, even though I wished we could walk and talk longer.

"Can I walk you to your car?" he asked.

My eyes widened and I suddenly felt even more surprised than I had the entire evening. He wasn't trying to pressure me into having a drink with him, or going back to his place, or anything else that every other guy would have done. I was impressed, to say the least.

"Well, where are you parked?" I asked him.

"I'm right around the corner in the parking garage," he explained. "Where's your car?"

"I parked five blocks away because I didn't want to pay for parking," I said with a chuckle.

"That's no problem. Let's go," he said, as he held out his elbow for me to hold onto.

"You really don't have to, Gabe. It's a long ways and it's pointless for you to walk me. It's not like I'm going to get mugged or something in this part of town. You don't have to take the hike with me."

"Nonsense," Gabe said, matter-of-factly. "I'm happy to walk with you. It's a nice night and it feels good to be outside."

A coy smirk crossed my face. *Is this what a real gentleman is like? Or did I die and wake up in a different era, where men actually treated women like princesses?*

I slipped my hand into the crease of his elbow and walked alongside him. My heart thumped in my chest as we made our way to my car. I wasn't sure how this date would come to a close. Would it be an awkward hug or would he just go straight for a kiss on the lips? It seemed like there wasn't much in between, at least in my experience.

We turned the final corner and I looked up to see my ancient car parked crooked in the street.

I really should learn to parallel park one of these days, I thought.

"That's my car, right up there," I said, lamely motioning towards my sad transportation.

We strolled up to it and I released Gabe's arm. The street

lamp above us shined down, causing his green eyes to glow. I once again found myself melting into them.

"Thank you for having dinner with me," he said. His voice was low and inviting. It made my insides turn just a little bit mushy.

"Well, thank you for taking me to dinner," I responded. "That place was amazing. Next time I might get the steak, though. That looked really good."

"Next time?" Gabe asked, smiling flirtatiously. My knees threatened to melt out from under me when he smiled like that.

I stuttered. "I mean, if I ever were to go there again for some reason. You know what I meant."

Gabe just chuckled softly. "I had a really great time tonight, Harper. To be honest, I was a little nervous before I met you. I've had some not-so-great dates with women. I was pleasantly surprised this time. This was a lot of fun."

"I had a really great time too," I said. And I meant it. It was the best date I had ever been on, and I had been on a lot of dates.

We stood close and Gabe's hands were on my sides. This was the part that always made me feel the most awkward, because typically this was when a guy would go in for a kiss and I'd have to turn away. But not this time. If Gabe went for a kiss, I was ready. I wanted that kiss.

He leaned in and I steadied myself, breathing in his intoxicating cologne. It was woodsy, yet had a clean scent that made me want more. He got close and then gave me a simple kiss on the cheek before pulling away.

"Drive safe, okay?" he said, taking a step back.

I was shocked.

That's it?

I had really hoped for more than just a kiss on the cheek

and my lips were practically puckered in expectation. I thought about kissing him again, this time the way that I wanted. But I didn't. Gabe was practically too good to be true and the last thing I wanted to do was to mess things up by acting too eager. So I just pulled my keys out of my purse and unlocked my car door.

Like the gentleman he clearly was, Gabe opened the door for me and I got into the seat.

"Thanks for dinner," I said, still not sure what was going on. This never happened to me.

"You're very welcome," he responded. "Can we do this again soon?"

"I'd like that."

He smiled and closed the door. I had no choice but to start up the car. The date was over, even though I wasn't really ready for it to be. When I pulled away from the curb, I looked into the rear view mirror. Gabe waved and then began walking back toward the restaurant, where his car was parked.

The whole drive home, I couldn't stop thinking about him. I was completely shocked. He hadn't tried to push me into anything. In fact, I was actually the one who wanted more. It was a surprising, yet refreshing end, to an already amazing date.

I knew that it had to be too good to be true.

CHAPTER 8

This is just writer's block, right? I mean, surely there was something about last night's date with Gabe that went terribly. There must be something for me to write about...

I sat in my office chair, staring at the blank screen of the word processing program in front of me. I had been gazing at it for half an hour, trying to brainstorm what to write for the upcoming blog post. The problem, though, was that I ran a website that people visited to hear about my *bad* dates, not the good ones. There wasn't anything interesting about a good date, or at least anything that my current readers would want to hear. They wanted the ridiculous details. They wanted the men who didn't pay for dinner and the ones who wore sweat pants to their first date. They didn't want to read about the charming, good-looking, gentlemanly Gabe.

I pressed my fingers against my cheek where he had kissed me. I could still feel the soft touch of his lips, and I could just imagine what they would feel like on mine. I wanted to feel them. I wanted so much more.

No words were coming through my fingers, no matter

how intently I stared at the screen. I needed to figure out the best way to approach the blog post about the date with Gabe and since staring at my computer wasn't helping, I decided to call up Cora for some advice.

I grabbed my cell phone and kicked my feet up onto the desk to give her a call. It rang three times before she finally picked up.

"Hey, lady," she said. "I hope you're calling to tell me about all of the juicy details from last night's date. I've been waiting patiently all morning. Please tell me that he showed up wearing a clown suit or something."

"I wish that had happened," I said.

"What do you mean?" she asked, interest flowing through her voice.

"The date was a disaster."

"That's great!" she replied. "I can't wait to read the hilarious blog post about it!"

"No, Cora. That's the problem." I set my feet on the floor. "The date was a disaster because it *wasn't* a disaster. It was actually a lot of fun."

She was silent for a moment before speaking up again. "Oh my, Harper. That sounds absolutely terrible."

I ignored her patronizing tone. "It was horrible! His name was Gabe. He was well-dressed, funny, charming and a total gentleman. He paid for dinner, walked me to my car and only wanted a kiss on the cheek to end the night."

"Harper, I want to feel sorry for you right now, but you have to understand how ridiculous this sounds. You're telling me that you had the date of a lifetime and yet, you sound like you're about to have an anxiety attack because of it."

"I know, it's insane," I said. "It's just that I wasn't

expecting it. And I still need to write this blog post, but now I don't know what to say."

"Tell the truth," she said, like it was the easy answer.

I thought about it for a moment, but then shrugged away the idea. If I blogged about the truth then it wouldn't be keeping with the horror-story theme of my blog. And if I lied, well then I'd be just painting the date as something it wasn't, and I didn't want to do that. It didn't seem right.

I started to wonder if I should just skip the blog post completely. I worried that a "bad" date post would somehow come back and bite me in the ass, potentially ruining any future possibilities with Gabe. I wanted to go on a second date with him.

"I don't know what to do, Cora," I said slowly. I picked up a pencil on my desk and spun it around through my fingers. "But I don't think I should spell out how amazing Gabe is on my blog. My readers don't want to hear about that kind of thing. You know that. They want bad dates."

"Harper, you need to look at this a different way. This was your very first date with him. People tend to put their best foot forward on a first date. Maybe that's all this was. Maybe he's not really quite as amazing as he made himself seem and somewhere underneath that gorgeous smile and charming demeanor, there's a crazy guy who deserves to be put on the wall of shame that you call your blog. Maybe he's got that slow-burning crazy, you know? The kind of crazy that takes a little while before it's revealed."

I chuckled. "What are you saying, Cora?"

"I'm saying that maybe all is not lost. Are you going on another date with... what was his name again? Abe?"

"It's Gabe." I was surprised at how I felt almost angry that she had gotten his name wrong.

"Are you going on another date with Gabe?" she asked.

"Nothing is set in stone yet, but he did ask if we could get together again soon and I said yes," I told her. "We only went on a date yesterday. I'm expecting him to follow the three day rule, so..."

"Perfect!" Cora announced. "Well then don't worry too much about the blog right now. Just relax and forget about it for the time being. You don't have to update it immediately. Instead, you should wait until you get a second date with Gabe and then when his inner craziness finally comes out, you'll have plenty of things to write about."

"You know, that's actually not a bad idea," I said slowly. I could see this post going well as long as he went crazy. The idea of him turning out to be awful was rather depressing, though..."

"You're welcome," Cora responded sarcastically. "I should start charging you for this advice."

"You might want to," I agreed. "Someday, I'll be rich and famous because of your ideas."

"Besides, even if Gorgeous Gabe doesn't end up wanting to see you again, there are plenty of fish in the sea who you can write about," Cora said. "In fact, don't you have another first date tonight with some other guy? I'm sure that one will be great fodder for your blog."

I quickly jumped up from my chair and glanced at the clock. I had been so focused on Gabe that I'd completely lost track of my other dates.

"Oh no!" I said. "I had completely forgotten about that! Cora, I've got to get ready. Thanks for the reminder."

Cora giggled. "No problem. Have fun with tonight's victim! I hope it goes terribly. And I mean that in the best possible way."

"Thanks, lady."

I hung up the phone and got undressed to take a shower.

My thoughts weren't really on my upcoming bowling date with this new guy, though. They were still on Gabe.

Calm down, Harper, I told myself. *You just had one date with the guy. Just because you haven't had a good date in years, doesn't mean you're going to marry the dude. Plus, like Cora said, there's a good chance he has some of that slow-burn crazy yet to reveal.*

With the thoughts of Gabe pushed to the back of my mind, I got ready for the evening. I only had about an hour before I had to meet this new guy at the bowling alley.

And this one was sure to be promising material for my blog. I just had a feeling.

CHAPTER 9

As if I wasn't already feeling rushed enough to get ready for a date with a stranger, my sister decided to stop by, unannounced. I had barely hopped out of the shower and squeezed into some skinny jeans before my doorbell sounded. I knew it was Rosie even before I went to the door. She was a surprise-visiting madwoman and the only one who would ever show up to my house without some kind of warning.

"I'm coming!" I shouted, as the doorbell continue to ring.

If she wasn't so obtrusive, I'd just give her a damn key to the house, I thought. I realized just how awful of an idea that would be. I'd have my mother and Rosie at my house constantly if they had free access. As much as I loved them both, I didn't think I could handle that.

I slipped on a simple blue blouse and then ran downstairs. My hair was still wet as it bounced over my shoulders. Sure enough, when I turned the corner, there was Rosie standing at the front door. She waved when she saw me.

"Hi, Rosie," I said as I unlocked the door and let her in.

"Jeez, Harper, what took you so long?" she asked. "I've been standing out here forever."

"I was in the shower," I responded. "I do have things to do, you know? Working from home doesn't mean that I'm never working."

"Well, that's why I came over," she said, as she pushed past me and made her way to the living room.

I closed the door and followed her, feeling my wet hair drip down my back as I moved. With my sister's visit, I doubted that I'd have time to dry and straighten it, so I basically just accepted that I'd have curly hair for this date. Rosie plopped down on my couch and kicked her feet up onto my coffee table.

"I noticed that you haven't updated your blog today," she said. "And it got me to wondering about your date last night."

"Oh yeah, last night's date," I mumbled. I'd meant to call her and tell her about it, but I wasn't quite ready for the 'I told you so' that I knew was going to come with it.

"Well, tell me everything," Rosie pried. "Was Gabe the man he claimed to be? Did he look like he did in the pictures? I hope he looked like his pictures. He was model material."

I rolled my eyes and chuckled softly to myself. "Yes, Rosie. He was the same guy as in the pictures. And actually, the date went really well. I was honestly kind of surprised by how fun it was."

"Really?" Rosie said, leaning forward. Well, as forward as she could with her belly. "You mean you *liked* him?"

"I said the *date* went well. I didn't say whether or not I *liked* him."

Even if I did like him, which I totally didn't, there was no way I was going to tell Rosie that. There was no way I was going to tell her that I thought he was charming and hand-some and had made me laugh all night long. She would just rub it in on how she knew best.

Rosie saw right through me, though. Her eyes widened with delight and she couldn't help but to let out a giggle. "I knew it! I *knew* it was going to work out with him. See, I'm the best matchmaker there is, Harper. You should have let me set you up all along."

"Rosie, I love you, but I think you're getting a little ahead of yourself," I said, pushing her feet off my coffee table and onto the floor a little roughly. "I mean it was only one date and just because it wasn't completely horrendous, doesn't necessarily mean that he qualifies as my future husband."

"I think you're playing it off as something much smaller than what it really is," she said as she twirled her hair with a pride-filled smile plastered on her face. "You haven't had a decent date in years, Harper. I mean, I just don't want you to screw this up like you did with Craig."

I cringed and felt a little burst of anger fill me as she spoke. I hated it when she brought up Craig. The relation-ship had fallen apart when he had taken a job overseas. The breakup wasn't my fault, but the hurt of that breakup still stung.

"First off, Rosie, that's entirely unfair to bring up my relationship with Craig." I did my best to keep my voice calm, even though I wanted to scream the words. "It's not even relevant to what we're talking about. Craig and I were finished years ago. He ended it. Not me."

"Right, that's my point, Harper," she said, ignoring the warning in my voice. "The last good date you had was with him. What have you been doing for the past three years? Seems to me like you've spent all your time going on bad dates. I was merely stating a fact. This date with

Gabe has been the first decent one you've had since Craig."

I was beginning to get legitimately annoyed. What she was saying wasn't wrong, but it was something that I already knew. There was no point in bringing it up and the only thing it was doing was making me look and feel bad.

"I don't want to talk about Craig or Gabe," I said firmly. "Change the subject."

Rosie didn't get the message. "Don't push Gabe away like you did Craig is all I'm saying." She shrugged as if it was entirely my fault that the relationship had fallen apart.

"Look, dating outside of college is infinitely harder. Once you start working, your circle of friends change. It's not the same." I snapped back, red filling my vision. "And not everyone can just marry *their boss.*"

The words fell out of my mouth and I immediately felt bad about saying them. It was definitely a sore spot for her.

Low blow, Harper. Put the claws away and leave your sister alone, I thought, putting my hand over my mouth. I immediately wished I hadn't said anything. Just because she was pushing my buttons didn't mean I needed to push back.

Rosie looked to the ground and I could tell that what I had said hit home for her. Her shoulders slumped. I took a calming breath, knowing that she was here because she loved me. I walked up and sat next to her on the couch, wrapping a loving arm over her shoulder.

"I didn't mean that," I said. "I'm sorry. It's just that, I know that I've had a rough few years of dating and it's hard to get reminded of it."

"I shouldn't have brought up Craig. I sounded like Mom," she admitted. "I think I've just been spoiling for a fight. I'm really sorry, Harper. It was mean of me. I'm going to blame hormones for this one."

I rolled my eyes. "You blame everything on hormones."

"It's one of the few perks of being pregnant." Rosie's defeated look quickly turned back into a hopeful smile. "I really am happy for you, though. It's good to hear that you had fun. Plus, you never know. Maybe Gabe will turn out to be something good. Like *really* good."

I shrugged. "Anything is possible." My eyes moved past her to the clock on the wall. It was almost seven. "Rosie, I'm sorry to do this, but I have about fifteen minutes before I need to be at the bowling alley."

"Are you going bowling with Gabe?" she asked, her smile giving away her excitement.

"No, it's a new guy," I explained, immediately wishing I had thought of saying anything else.

"Really?" Her face fell. "But I thought things with Gabe went well?"

"I already told you, sis. The date went well with Gabe, but that doesn't mean I have to put my entire dating life on hold because of it." I gave her a hug and offered her my hand to get off the couch. "Besides, I have to have bad dates to put up on the blog. This date is just for work."

Rosie eyed me warily for a moment before taking my hand. She grunted with the effort of standing as she followed me to the door.

"Just for work, huh?" Rosie let out a long suffering sigh as I slid on my shoes. "I suppose that's fine. But if you really like Gabe, you shouldn't do anything that could screw it up. Be careful with this guy."

I walked through the front door with Rosie close behind as she followed me out. I hoped that my hair would be dry by the time I got to the bowling alley. "I won't screw anything up. I'm a dating pro, remember?"

"Are you sure you should go on this date?" she asked as I

locked the door behind us. "You could call and cancel right now. Maybe go on a date with Gabe instead?"

"Good night, Rosie," I said, as I gave her a quick hug and hopped in my car. "I'll give you a call tomorrow and tell you all about tonight's date. Or you can just read about it on my blog tomorrow night. I have a feeling it's going to make for a great story."

CHAPTER 10

The moment I laid my eyes on Dave, I knew that this was going to be a date that would result in an awesome blog post. He was standing next to his car in the parking lot of the bowling alley. The car looked like it probably belonged to his grandma. It was one of those giant olive-green boats that I would see old women driving while their white hair bounced just above the steering wheel.

Dave, my date for the evening, was leaning against this car like it was the coolest thing on four wheels. He looked proud while wearing a two-tone bowling shirt and khaki-colored slacks, which actually made the car look pretty good in contrast. His blonde hair was combed over to the side and he smiled goofily as soon as I walked up.

"You must be the lovely Harper," he said, flashing me a friendly smile.

"And you must be Dave." I went for a handshake but he ignored it and pulled me in for a hug. My face hit his chest and a scent entered my nose. It was the smell of cheap cologne attempting to hide body odor. It wasn't pleasant, to say the least.

"Do you have your bowling shoes?" he asked, looking around like I had an invisible bag somewhere on the ground.

"Um, I don't actually own bowling shoes," I responded.

"What about a ball?" He was still looking for my invisible bowling gear. "Do you have your own ball?"

This is off to a great start, I thought. *A great start for my blog...*

"No, I'm not really a bowler, so I don't have any of that stuff." I shrugged and offered up a smile. "I guess I'll have to rent."

"I *guess* that will work," he said, as he popped the trunk of his car and grabbed a fancy looking bag out of the back. "Are you ready to do some bowling then?"

I sighed and glanced back at my car, kind of thinking I'd rather just leave. But then I remembered that I still needed something good to write about on my blog. This date had "nightmare" written all over it so I couldn't just run away.

"Yeah, let's bowl," I said, as I mustered up all of the excitement that I possibly could.

Dave wrapped an arm over my shoulder and we walked into the bowling alley. I took the first chance I could to get away from him and walked up to the counter to rent my shoes.

"I'll go get a lane," he said. "I'll meet you over there. Get ready to have some fun!"

It took absolutely everything in my power to keep my eyes from rolling. But I managed, then turned to the counter and rented my shoes. After slipping them on, I walked down toward lane ten, where Dave was standing and polishing his bowling ball like it was a precious historical artifact. I took notes in my mind. I wanted to remember all of this.

Pure gold, I thought. *I don't know if it gets much better than this.*

By the time I approached him, he had put on some sort of wrist brace.

"What's that for?" I asked, nodding to his wrist.

"I use this to keep from injuring my wrist," he explained. "This isn't my lucky one since I'm not competing with you. I'm a professional bowler, you know? This baby is how I make my bread and butter."

He held his right arm up, with a proud expression on his face. You'd have thought that arm had cured cancer by the way he looked. It certainly hadn't said that on his profile.

"Interesting," I humored him. "A professional bowler, huh?"

Well, now I know for a fact that I'm going to lose this game.

"Yeah. It's not all glory, though," he explained, as he punched some things into the ancient bowling computer. The end of the lane lit up and the pins were revealed.

"No?" I had always thought bowling was just a fun game. I never really considered it a professional sport with *glory.*

"The touring around, the women, the fame, sometimes it's just a lot to handle," he continued, nonchalantly striking a heroic pose. "I'm rather important on the circuit. I'm kind of a big deal. I'm surprised you haven't heard of me."

I waited for the wink or nod to indicate it was a joke, but it never came. I snorted as I held back a laugh. He was serious. I couldn't believe it. I didn't even own bowling shoes-how would I have ever heard of him?

"Anyway, get yourself a ball and let's get rolling," he said. "Tell you what, if you beat me, then I'll buy you dinner."

Thank God I'm going to lose this game, I thought. *I do not want to go to dinner and listen to bowling hero stories.*

I grabbed a ball and walked back to the lane, setting my ball down in the holder.

"You're up," Dave said, motioning to my resting ball.

"You want me to go first?"

"Ladies first." He grinned widely. I grimaced as I saw that he had missed a spot brushing his teeth.

With a sigh, I walked up and attempted a roll. The ball made it about three quarters of the way down the lane before sinking in the gutter. I turned around and walked back to my seat, ignoring Dave's look of disappointment.

"I'm not much of a bowler," I admitted.

"Your profile said that you like sports," he replied, putting his hands on his hips.

"I do like sports. Like football," I explained.

He frowned for a moment. "Then you probably should have checked that option instead of just sports. Sports means a lot of things."

It was one of the answers that I had changed from Rosie's answers about me. Had one little exaggeration changed my match that much? No way was the software *that* good.

"It's not a problem, though," he said, a knowing grin spreading across his face. "Let me show you how it's done. I can teach you so much."

Oh please do, almighty bowler. Grace me with your skills, awe me with your God-given talent, I thought.

This was going to be the easiest blog post I'd ever written. I watched Dave stroll up the lane. He held his bowling ball up to his lips and gently kissed it, before doing his roll. The ball hit the lane and spun, giving it the perfect arch at cruised down toward the pins. It hit perfectly and exploded into his first strike of the game. He turned around, nodding his head and smiling as he walked and sat down next to me.

"Just like that," he said. "That's all you have to do."

"That easy, huh?" I said. I smiled and batted my eyelashes a little to flirt. "I have this feeling that you're going to win this game."

"Most likely," he responded without even a pause. Arrogance rippled off him in waves.

Wow. I thought to myself. *What a charmer.*

I glanced up at the bowling lights. We still had nine more frames of torture. I wanted to just thank him and see if I could return my shoes and still get my money back, but I couldn't just leave. This was the best fodder for my website that I had had in a while. This date was like a payday for me and I needed it. So I got up and rolled another ball. This one made it almost all the way down the lane before it sunk in the gutter. I felt like I was getting better.

Dave hopped up and of course rolled another strike right after me. He was just beginning a celebratory dance when my phone vibrated in the front pocket of my jeans.

Thank God. Maybe my house is on fire and I can go home, I thought.

Any excuse to look at my phone was welcomed. I thought for sure it would be Cora or my sister, so I was surprised to see an unknown number. I normally didn't answer calls like that, but this was an exception. Dave walked up to give me a high five right as I answered the call.

"Sorry, this is for work," I told Dave before putting the phone up to my ear. "Hello?"

"Is this Harper?" A man's voice asked.

"Yes, this is she," I replied.

Dave stood in front of me with his arms cross. He whispered, "We're on a date. You should get off the phone."

I held up my hand and smiled. I *did* just say it was for work. We couldn't all be professional bowlers.

"Hi. It's Gabe, from last night." The voice filled with an obvious smile on the other side of the line.

"Gabe?" My heart flop flopped to the sound of his voice. I was a little surprised to hear from him. I didn't expect him to defy the three-day rule for calling me. It had hardly been twenty-four hours since I had seen him last. "Hi."

"It's kind of loud where you are," he said. "I can't hear you very well."

"I'm sorry, I'm at a bowling alley," I explained. I took a step away from the lanes and up onto a carpeted area where it was marginally quieter. "How are you? I'm actually glad you called."

"I'm doing well, I just wanted to touch base and see if you were free this weekend. I got an extra ticket for a certain game of a certain team, and I thought that you might like to come with me."

"You have tickets to the Blue Jays?" I squealed, as my eyes lit up with excitement.

Dave was still standing in front of me, looking totally annoyed, but I didn't care. I had just received some pretty amazing news. If a bowling strike was worthy of a celebratory dance, this was worthy of a whole dance party.

"Yep, I've got two tickets and I'd love it if you could join me," Gabe said. "If not, I understand. It's pretty short notice."

"Are you kidding me? Count me in! I'm not going to miss the chance to see my team play at home," I exclaimed. "That doesn't come around very often for me."

"Good," he said. "The game is at six. I am unfortunately in meetings until about five, but I can come to pick you up right after."

"I don't want you to have to rush to my place after your

meeting just to pick me up," I replied. "Why don't we just meet at the stadium?"

"That works for me," he said. "I'll see you then. I'm looking forward to it."

"Me too, Gabe." I was all smiles and my stomach was doing happy flip-flops. "I'll see you on Sunday. It's a date."

I hung up the phone and slipped it back into my pocket. I was beaming and I had a giant grin from ear to ear. I had almost forgotten where I was, standing in the bowling alley with Dave.

"Did you just plan a date with whoever you were on the phone with?" he asked. "That didn't exactly sound like work."

Even though dating was kind of technically my job, I wasn't going to flat out lie, so I just shrugged. "Yeah, I guess I did."

"Are you kidding me?" He threw his hands up in the air dramatically. "Who does that?"

"Sorry, Dave," I said, feeling a little sheepish. The rudeness of what I had just done was slowly dawning on me. "I just had a chance to go to a football game on Sunday and I took the offer. We can still finish our game of bowling, though."

"No way. This is ridiculous," he said, as he walked over and grabbed his ball, stuffing it into his bag. He kicked off his bowling shoes and threw them in with the ball with a flourish.

"I'm sorry, Dave," I said, watching him have a mini temper tantrum with his things. "This clearly wasn't meant to be, though. I think we can both agree on that."

"You're telling me," he responded. "You don't even *bowl*."

I stared after him as he marched past me and out the front doors of the building. The effect was somewhat ruined when he stopped at the announcement board on his way out and signed up for a tournament. Apparently, I hadn't devastated him too badly.

I looked down at my shoes and started to chuckle. *I* was the bad date this time. I was the one who deserved to be written up and skewered for bad behavior on a date. My laughter started to come louder as the irony of being the bad date took hold.

Some of the other bowlers must have thought I'd lost my mind. I returned the bowling shoes and went to my car, noticing that the olive green Dave-mobile wasn't there any more. He had gotten out of there in a hurry. My old car was still parked crooked, just like last night.

That's when it hit me.

This is how I can write about a good date and a bad date in one blog post, I realized. *My good date with Gabe has turned me into the worst first date.*

I hurried home, anxious to tell the world how *I* was the worst date ever.

CHAPTER 11

Okay, Harper. Keep it together. It's just a football game with a guy, I told myself. *Your eyebrows don't need to look perfect. Just take a breath.*

I was still in my car, checking myself out in the rear view mirror. I hadn't felt this nervous for a date in a long time. Every time I looked in the mirror, I saw a little blemish on my skin or a hair out of place. I felt like I had lost my mind.

"This is insane," I whispered. "He's not going to even notice my eyebrows."

It was time to meet him. I'd gotten here early and just sat in my car stressing for the past fifteen minutes and now I was technically late. It was my first second date in a very, very long time. I wasn't sure what the etiquette was.

This must be how most people feel on first dates, I thought to myself.

With a deep breath, I pulled my Blue Jays' cap onto my head and stepped out of the car. I could already hear the crowd inside, roaring with excitement. This wasn't just a regular game. This was one of *the* biggest games of the year.

Our rival team, The Crows, had flown down from Maine to try to obtain victory on our turf.

Gabe was standing at the front entrance as I walked up. He was wearing a bright-colored Blue Jays' jersey and jeans. He filled out the jersey nicely in the shoulders. On his head was a well-loved blue baseball cap similar to mine. My eyes lit up when I saw him, and the beating in my chest increased.

Calm down, Harper. You have to play this cool, I reminded myself.

His smile and green eyes pulled me toward him. It felt like I wasn't even walking across the parking lot. It was more like floating.

"Hey!" he said as I neared. "I'm glad you made it."

I strolled up and wrapped my arms around Gabe's neck to give him a hug. The smell of his cologne hit my nose, causing me to smile. It was hard not to take a deep breath in of him. "There's no way I'd miss this," I told him with a grin. "Sorry I'm late, though."

"It's no problem," he said with a grin. "We still have a few minutes before kickoff."

"Let's hurry!" I exclaimed. "We can't miss kickoff. I'm superstitious like that. I'm always afraid that we'll lose if I don't see the kickoff."

Gabe chuckled and then reached down to take my hand, walking me into the stadium. As we took the escalator toward the top, he reached into his other pocket and pulled out the tickets, handing me one.

"Thank you for inviting me along," I said, as I glanced down at the ticket. My eyes widened when I saw it. I wasn't sure what I was expecting, but I sort of figured we'd have average seats for the game. Maybe not nose bleeders, but possibly middle of the road. I almost choked when I saw that they were actually box seats.

"You're kidding me," I whispered, as I looked back to Gabe. "Box seats?"

"Yeah, well, sometimes there are some perks to my job," he said, shrugging like it was nothing.

A software engineer gets box seats one of the most important, and expensive, games of the season? I asked myself. *He must be doing something right, because these tickets are easily worth over a thousand bucks a piece. This guy has money, there's no doubt about it.*

"I never thought I'd get to go to this game," I said, as we reached the top of the escalator and handed our tickets to the stadium employee. "Let alone have box seats!"

"You're in for a treat then," Gabe said with a laugh. "After you watch a game like this, you won't be able to do it any other way."

We took another elevator up and then walked through the crowd of people surrounding the hot dog and beer stands. Finally, we got to a set of stairs that took us to the box seating. We had to show our ticket stubs to a different stadium employee, who let us into the small room with leather seats.

As soon as I stepped inside, I felt a blast of air conditioning flow over me. Considering the heat outside, it felt luxurious. I could see the thousands of screaming fans through the giant windows all melting with the evening heat, and I knew that it wasn't the norm.

There were only about ten seats comfortably spaced through the large room and all of them were filled with Blue Jay fans, except for the two in the middle. These seats looked rich and comfortable, especially compared to the plastic ones outside.

"Those are ours," Gabe said, leading me to the seats.

We sat down and I took a second to look around. I couldn't believe this was actually happening. A week ago I was on a date and getting stiffed with the bill and then here I was, getting spoiled with amazing seats at a football game. Maybe Rosie was right. Maybe there really could be a future with Gabe.

I shook these thoughts out of my mind for the moment, though, reminding myself that it was just date number two and that I still didn't really know him. I needed to not get ahead of myself.

A waitress approached within a minute of us sitting down. We both ordered a beer and while we waited, I stood up and approached the window which took up the entire wall. Every inch of the field was visible. The view was so good that I could practically see the football players' expressions as they lined up for the national anthem. My team was wearing bright blue jerseys with white pants, and the Crows were wearing all black.

"This is absolutely incredible," I whispered. It was even better than watching the game on TV.

Gabe stepped up beside me and placed a hand on my lower back. I loved the way his hand felt, and I hoped he never stepped away.

"What do you think?" he asked.

"I think that you were right when you said I'd never be able to watch a game any other way again." I said, looking up at him and smiling. "This is amazing, Gabe. Thank you so much for this."

"Only thank me if we win," he said, using his free hand to tug on his ballcap. The motion looked almost nervous.

"Oh, we're going to win," I assured him. "I have my lucky hat on, so there's no way we can lose this game."

"And I have my lucky jersey on," he replied, plucking at his blue jersey. "So between the two of us, there's not a single possibility that we could lose."

"Is that a Peyton Boyying jersey?" I asked, admiring his jersey.

He nodded. "My favorite player."

"One of these days I'm going to buy a real jersey," I said, feeling a little envious. A Peyton Boyying jersey would be a dream jersey. "Maybe when they don't cost a hundred and fifty dollars anyway."

Gabe smiled as he looked down at his shirt. "Yeah, they're a little overpriced. But you know, if it brings us enough luck to win today's game, then it'll be worth every penny."

Before I could respond, the waitress came back up with our beers. We took our seats once again and held our beers in the air.

"To the Jays!" I said.

Everyone else in the box seats shouted it back with excitement. I blushed, not realizing how loud I had been with my cheers. It was easy to forget everyone else when Gabe was around.

"At least everyone here is a fan for the right team," Gabe said, as he clinked his plastic cup against mine.

A man sitting behind us reached forward and squeezed Gabe's shoulder. "Good to see you, Gabe. Glad you could make it."

We turned around to see a familiar face, one that I had see a hundred times on TV. It was Oscar Demoya, the owner of the Blue Jays.

No freaking way, I thought, trying really hard not to stare. This *is the owner's box? How in the heck did Gabe pull this one off?*

"Good to see you, too, Oscar," Gabe said, as he shook the man's hand. "I'm ready to see the Jays pull this one off. It's an important game. If we win this one then there's a chance we clinch the division."

"I've got a good feeling," Oscar replied. "Our defense is stronger than ever before. If our offense can't pull it off, I know our defense can."

"I totally agree," Gabe responded. "Defense is on point. Looking forward to see the Crows lose."

He turned back to face me and I was pretty sure my expression said it all.

"That's the owner," Gabe whispered with a wink.

"I know," I said.

But jeez, I didn't know you were buddies with him.

A few seconds later, I brought my attention through the glass, watching as The Crows kicked off. The Jays received and the game started with a twenty-seven yard return.

"That's what I'm talking about!" I shouted, getting into the game. It all felt too surreal, so the only thing I could do was enjoy it.

I gave Gabe a high five and sat back down. Gabe was smiling ear to ear.

"You weren't kidding when you said you were a football fan," he said. "I was afraid you were just feeding me a line."

"I'm just getting started," I replied. "Just wait until fourth quarter. You may regret bringing me."

Gabe laughed. "I don't think there's a possibility of me regretting anything with you."

The game continued and it wasn't long before both Gabe and I were standing up in our seats, clapping and cheering to nearly every play. We had the entire box riled up, with the exception of the few older friends of Oscar's. They just smiled and laughed at our foolish antics. I realized that I was probably embarrassing myself with my excitement over a football game, but I refused to change the way I watched football for anyone. And luckily, Gabe was just as into it as I was.

Halftime approached quickly and the score was seven to three, with the Crows leading.

"Apparently my hat and your jersey aren't helping the team out with any luck," I said, before taking a sip from my second beer. "What else can we do?"

"I don't even know," Gabe said, with a defeated look on his face. "I guess we just hope that the Blue Jays show up to play in the second half. They're looking terrible out there."

We stood next to each other, just watching the last play of the first half. I was a little upset about how the game was going, but it was more than made up for by my joy of being there with Gabe. Everything about him was perfect. On most of my previous dates, I'd watch the time drag on as I waited for it to end. But this evening was flying by so quickly, which honestly bummed me out. I didn't want the night to be over any time soon.

"Do you want to watch the halftime show?" I asked, as the first half came to a close. "I hate that they never show them on TV."

"I agree," Gabe said with an enthusiastic nod. "Before I forget, though, I wanted to ask you if you were interested in doing something special with me after the game."

"Special?" I frowned, wondering what he could possibly have in mind. "Like what?"

"I was wondering if you'd want to go down and meet some of the players," he said nonchalantly. "I can get us an access pass and we can meet them before they enter the locker room. We can probably get your hat signed too."

I stood in silence for a moment, quieted by my complete shock.

"I mean we don't have to. Only if you want," Gabe said quickly. "I just thought, maybe-"

"Are you joking?" I interrupted him. "Yes! Yes, that is absolutely something I want to do! It just took me a second to compute what you were saying!"

And I thought this date couldn't get any better, I thought. *Now he's telling me he'll take me to meet some of the players! This has to be a dream.*

"Perfect, we'll go down once the game is over," he said, a relieved smile filling his face.

He wrapped an arm over my shoulder and I leaned into him as we watched the halftime show. My eyes were looking at the field the entire time, but my mind was focused only on the amazing man standing next to me.

Don't pee yourself, Harper. Try to keep your tongue in your mouth. Don't get ahead of yourself.

This might be the best day of your life, let alone date, but he still might turn out to be crazy.

CHAPTER 12

*E*verything Gabe had promised me had come true. He had gotten an access pass from Oscar, which allowed us downstairs to an area just outside of the Blue Jay's locker room. I was able to meet almost all of my favorite players and had even gotten my hat signed by Peyton Boyying.

"I can't believe the Jays were able to make a comeback," I said, as Gabe walked me across the parking lot to my car. I held my signed hat in my hand, admiring the scribble of permanent ink that the quarterback had left on the bill.

"I knew they'd come to play in the second half," he replied. "They're always stronger after halftime."

"I know, but it's hard to put faith in that," I said, tracing the signature with my finger. "I was pretty nervous until we threw that last touchdown."

We approached my car and I suddenly felt a sinking feeling. The date was coming to an end. I wasn't ready for it to be over, though. I was still buzzing from an exciting evening. It wasn't even just the game. It was being with Gabe.

"Do you feel like maybe getting a drink and a snack somewhere?" I asked. "I'm kind of hungry."

That was a bit of a stretch, being that I had been eating pretzels and peanuts for most of the game. But I needed an excuse to spend more time with Gabe.

"I'd like that," he agreed with an easy smile. "There's a great little café about a block from here. They serve late meals. I'm pretty sure they stay open until midnight."

"Sounds perfect!" Relief flooded my chest. I didn't have to go home yet. I still had more time to spend with him.

We left my car and walked to the nearby café. It was fairly crowded, since the game had just ended, but we were able to get seated at the far end of the bar. The entire place was filled with energy as the celebration for the big win ensued. We sat down and ordered a drink, along with some appetizers.

"Thank you again for taking me to the game, Gabe," I told him. "I still can't believe how much fun it was."

My mind was still whirling from the excitement of meeting the players and I had to consciously calm myself down to keep from acting like a fool in front of Gabe. I felt like an excited kid on her birthday and if I let my feelings go, I'd have been jumping up and down.

"I'm really glad you were able to come with me tonight," said Gabe, after taking a sip from his beer. "It was definitely a lot more fun with you there."

"Sorry if I was acted a little crazier than you thought I would. But I warned you that I was a huge football fan when we first met." I shrugged and gave him a sheepish smile.

"I actually *love* how big of a fan you are," he replied. "I thought *I* was the biggest football nut until tonight's game. You might actually have me beat on that one."

I giggled and playfully pushed his shoulder. He reached

over and tickled me, just above my hips in reciprocation. This was flirting how it was meant to be and I loved it. It was fantastic.

"Based on your football obsession, I assume that you're in a fantasy league?" Gabe inquired.

I swirled my vodka cranberry in the glass, then took a sip from the straw before replying. "I'll be honest with you. I've never played."

"You've never played fantasy football?" he asked, in disbelief.

"No. I never really knew what it was or how it worked, so I didn't bother," I explained. "My coworkers at one of my old jobs did a fantasy league one year, but I didn't do it because I had no clue how to play. It seemed more complicated than the actual game."

Gabe's eyes lit up with excitement. "Oh my gosh, Harper. You have to play. It makes watching the games even more fun, since you have your own money on the line."

I thought back to the game, wondering how in the heck watching football could be any more fun than that.

"Well, how does it work?" I asked.

I couldn't help but to smile at his expression of excitement. He seemed so eager to tell me all about it that I would have listened to him explain just about anything.

"Okay, well there are a few different types of leagues. Some of them let you pick a full team to play with and others make you pick individual players for your team," he explained. "You can pick any players that are available from any roster in the professional league. You literally build your entire team from scratch."

My ears perked up a bit, though I was mostly just admiring the way he looked and how sweet he was. His smile was making it difficult to pay attention to the details of what he described.

"See, everything the players do in a game is worth a certain number of points. When a quarterback throws a touchdown, that's worth a few. When a defensive end gets a tackle, that's worth points also." His hand moved through the air in his excitement, and his smile lit up his face.

"Okay," I said, nodding encouragingly. It was impossible not to be caught up by his enthusiasm.

"At the end of every game, the points are added up and whoever has the most wins that round. So you've got to pick the right players and build the right team. But honestly, it sounds like you know enough about football to make it happen."

He smiled at me and I nearly melted into a happy puddle. Those green eyes made me feel like the most important person in the world.

"I *do* know a fair amount about the game, I guess," I admitted.

"I saw you calling out those plays tonight," Gabe said. "You know a whole lot more than you're admitting."

"You might be right," I agreed, sipping on my drink.

He had no idea how right he was. Six months out of the year, for my entire youth, I had sat with my dad and watched football growing up. I knew every play, every penalty, and practically every player. It was the thing I did with my dad and some of the best childhood memories I had.

"I *am* right," Gabe went on. "I can't wait to get you started on the league I'm in. You're going to love it, Harper. It makes the games more personal and more fun."

"Does it cost money?" I asked, as I thought about my

small bank account, which was probably walking the line of overdraft.

"It costs a little bit, but I'll cover you," he said. "I want you to play."

The more I thought about it, the more I realized that it actually sounded a whole lot more fun than I had ever given it credit for. I was still hesitant, but I was beginning to see the appeal. "I don't know..."

"Please, Harper. Let me get you in the game." He smiled encouragingly. "You can pay me back when you win all the games."

"Deal," I said after a moment. It probably wasn't much to get in, but I appreciated the gesture.

We held our glasses together and then took another sip. Our knees touched accidentally and out of reflex, I almost pulled away. But then I realized that I liked it. I *liked* sitting close to him like that. So I slid a little closer, causing Gabe to place his hand onto the top of my knee.

"You know what's crazy?" Gabe asked.

Please don't tell me it's you, I thought, half-jokingly to myself.

"What's that?" I responded.

"I'm in my thirties and you're the first woman I've ever met who I feel like I can talk to about this stuff." He laughed at himself.

"What stuff?" I asked. "Fantasy football?"

"That's part of it, definitely. But not all of it," he said. "It's just that most girls I've gone out with have always given me the impression that I needed to be somebody I wasn't, like I needed to build myself up just to please them. But you make me feel like I can let down my guard a little bit and just be myself, you know?"

"I actually know exactly what you mean," I replied.

"Really?" He sounded surprised.

"Yes, absolutely. I've been having a lot of fun with you, Gabe," I told him. I shrugged, trying not to make it a big deal. "I know this is just the second date, but I'm really enjoying this. I won't go into stories, but let's just say these dates with you are the best I've had in some time."

Gabe's lips curled up into a pleased smile. "Good. That makes me happy."

That was remarkably straightforward, I thought. *Is this how grownups do dating? I could definitely get used to this. It seems so easy and drama-free.*

We finished our drinks and appetizers, watching the crowd as it finally died down from the excitement of the game.

"It's almost eleven," Gabe said, glancing at his watch and looking surprised. "I should probably let you go home."

"It's that late already?" I asked. I couldn't believe how quickly the evening had gone by. I wished I had the ability to stop time and just stay in this comfortable moment for just a little bit longer.

"I'm just as surprised as you are," he admitted. "I completely lost track of time."

"Yeah, I suppose we should get out of here," I said. "I need to try to be productive tomorrow."

"Are you busy with a magazine article?" Gabe asked.

"Just working on some general writing. I've got to keep at it or else I get rusty," I said, tripping slightly on my words as I realized that bringing up my line of work probably wasn't the best idea. It was a vague but decent enough response. "But, it does need to be done."

"I'll walk you back to your car," he offered.

~

GABE THREW a couple twenty-dollar bills down on the table to cover our drinks and appetizers, and then took my hand as we stepped outside. The evening had gotten cool, causing a shiver to shoot up through my body.

"Are you cold?" Gabe asked.

Me being me, I couldn't admit to being cold or hurt or tired or anything else that showed weakness.

"No, I'm good," I replied, doing my best to keep from rubbing my arms.

"Well, I'm cold, so keep me warm," Gabe joked, as he wrapped an arm around me and pulled me close. I snuggled into him, loving the way he radiated warmth.

We walked like this back to the stadium parking lot. Each breath I took I could smell his cologne as it wafted off of his chest. It reminded me of our first date and the kiss on the cheek he had given me at the end of it. I hoped I could get a real kiss this time.

My car sat lonely in the parking lot, illuminated by a single street lamp. It was a little creepy and I was very glad that Gabe was with me to keep me safe. The stadium was in a decent area of town, but this late at night was never a good idea for a woman to walk around by herself. I pulled my keys out of my pocket as we approached, feeling the familiar end-of-date tension.

"Well, here we are," I said, wishing I had better words and less nerves.

Gabe faced me, placing his hands on my sides. "This was fun," he said.

"Yes. *So* much fun," I agreed. "Thank you so much for today."

The streetlights lit up his happy grin. It was infectious when he smiled like that.

"Can I see you again soon?" he asked, his voice cracking slightly at the end.

Are you freaking kidding me? Yes! Of course you can! Call me every day! Let's go out tomorrow, I thought.

"Yeah, I think that'd be okay," I said calmly, doing my best to hold back my enthusiasm. Inside, I was doing cartwheels and happy dances.

"Perfect." He paused for a moment, but didn't move. "Well, have a good night. I'll see you soon."

"Goodnight," I replied. I didn't move either. My heart hammered in my chest and I wondered just how pink my cheeks had to be. I was having a hard time breathing I was so nervous and excited for this moment.

Gabe leaned in. He didn't kiss my cheek this time, though, he brought his lips straight to mine. A burst of electricity filled the air, exploding all around us. His kiss took my breath away and my knees went weak. I brought my hands to his shoulders and pulled myself closer to him.

I had one hand around the back of his neck and the other on his cheek, feeling his stubble as it grazed my fingertips. Gabe slowly pulled away, looking at me with those beautiful green eyes. Then he kissed me again, this time with even more passion. A soft moan escaped my throat as he pulled my body against his.

Our lips parted and our tongues dashed in and out of each other's mouths, filling me from head to toe with a tingling sensation. My heart was beating quickly now, filled with eagerness and lust. Every emotion and desire of the evening flowed through me. My hands moved across his face, pulling him as closely as possible. It was like I couldn't get enough of him. I had spent so much time on bad dates and in bad relationships, and this one kiss was breaking the dam, allowing all of my passion to flow out of me.

I could have kissed him like this for hours. Days. Months. I could have kissed him like this forever and never have grown tired of it. But, we had to come up for air eventually.

Gabe slowly broke our kiss. I was practically panting and beyond turned on. If we hadn't been out in the parking lot, I'd probably have ripped off his clothes right there. "That might have been the best goodnight kiss I've ever had," he whispered. He sounded just as breathless as I felt.

The light above us illuminated the green of his eyes as he spoke. My hands were trembling as I gripped his muscular shoulders.

"No kidding," I agreed, still trying to catch my breath.

I expected him to ask me back to his place. I expected him to kiss me again, to press me against the hood of my car and show me what he was looking for. Instead of taking advantage of me in my vulnerable state of excitement, he gave me one more peck on the lips and then opened my car door for me.

"Best date ever," he said. He grinned and fixed his baseball cap so it fit on his head better. "I look forward to the next one."

I bit the corner of my bottom lip, as I kept myself from jumping him right there and having my way with him. I wasn't expecting him to be a gentleman and I wasn't sure how to react.

"Definitely," I said slowly. I didn't know what else to do but get in my car. Gabe closed the door for me and patted the top of my trunk as he walked away, leaving me filled with a combination of emotion unlike any other. He could have had his way with me right there. All he had to do was invite me to his place and I would have been out of those jeans in a heartbeat, allowing this amazing man to take me.

But he *didn't* do that. He respected me enough to let our second date end with just an amazing kiss, knowing that there would be more dates down the road.

If anything, it made me like him even more.

The smile on my face felt permanent as I drove home in the dark. It felt like I had finally met a man who knew how to treat a lady and I decided that I'd do whatever I possibly could to make sure that I didn't screw it up.

This time, I wanted neither of us to be the bad date.

CHAPTER 13

"Harper, you sound awfully cheery this morning," Mom said within thirty seconds of me answering the phone. "Tell me what's on your mind."

"What do you mean, Mom?" I asked, trying to sound innocent. "I sound the same as I always do."

"Not true," she disagreed. I could almost see her shaking her head through the phone.

"Maybe it was the extra cup of coffee I had this morning," I offered. "You know what caffeine does to me."

"Come on, Harper. I know you better than you know yourself," she informed me. "Tell me everything."

It had to be mother's intuition. She had the distinct ability to sense change in any and every inflection in my voice. No matter how hard I tried to sound "normal", the fact remained that I actually *was* a little more cheery than I'd usually be at nine in the morning. The date with Gabe the night before still had me wired. All that I could think about was the incredible kiss we had shared in the stadium parking lot.

"Harper, are you there?"

My mom's voice pulled me away from my idle daydreaming. I sat in my office chair with my fist under my chin, gazing out of the window, just lost in the memory of the night before.

"Yeah, sorry," I said. A soft smile filled my face and I could smell his cologne if I closed my eyes.

"See, I can tell your thoughts are elsewhere," she said. "Now spill it, Harper. Tell me everything before I have to pry it out of Rosie."

Mom is nothing if not persistent, I thought. *I suppose I can't get too frustrated with her, though. God knows I can be the same way if I really want something.*

"Okay, okay," I replied. "What do you want to know?"

"Rosie already told me you had your second date with Gabe last night, so I want to know how it went," she finally admitted. "Give me the details."

Darn it, Rosie, I thought. *Why do you have to gossip with Mother?*

There was definitely no turning back on the conversation at this point. So I just went ahead and jumped in headfirst.

"Yes, Gabe and I went on another date last night," I said simply. I wasn't about to offer up any more details. Especially not to my mother.

"And?" Mom pried.

"And, what?" I asked. "I just went on a date."

"Come on, Harper. Don't be like this." Mom was frowning at me through the phone. I could feel it. "The only reason I'm asking is because I'm excited for you, that's all. What did you guys do? Did he take you to another expensive restaurant or what?"

I chuckled at the last question. "No overpriced restaurant this time. But he actually did one better. You'll never guess where he took me."

"He took you shopping at Tiffany's?" Mom asked, her voice getting squeaky with excitement.

"No, Mom. That's where he would take *you* on a date." I rolled my eyes. "He got us box seats at the Blue Jays game, Mom. Can you believe that? Not just any box seats, though. We sat in the owner's box."

"You're joking," she replied. "That's not a date!"

"Nope, not kidding," I informed her. "Oscar Demoya sat behind us the entire time. The *owner* of the Blue Jays gave me high fives whenever the team scored a touchdown."

"What kind of date is that?" Mom asked, clearly not understanding why I was so happy. "He took you to a foot-ball game? That's not a date with a girl! That's something you do with your guy friends. He needs to take you out shopping. Or to a movie..."

I shook my head and only half listened to my mother rant about what a horrible date idea a football game was. I didn't care. A smile crossed my face and I closed my eyes, reliving the memory from the night before. Instantly, I could feel the excitement of the game again and the butterflies in my stomach from my crush on Gabe. I thought about his green eyes and smile, his smell and the way he tasted when we kissed.

My thoughts were broken, though, this time not by my mother but by a knock on my front door. I opened my eyes and sat up in my office chair.

"Hey, Mom, can I call you back?" I interrupted her. She was talking about proper foot apparel for dates now and how cleats just wouldn't cut it. "Someone's at the door."

"Just go see who it is. I'll wait," she responded with an exasperated sigh.

"Okay, hold on." I set the phone down and ran downstairs to see the deliveryman walking away from the front door. Sitting on my small patio was a cardboard box. I stepped out and grabbed it, then spun around, using my foot to close the door.

"What's this?" I wondered out loud. "I'm not expecting any packages."

My mom was still on hold upstairs, but I wasn't in a huge rush to continue her lecture of how a sporting event wasn't a real date, so I grabbed some scissors from the kitchen drawer and used them to cut the tape on the box. When I opened it up, the first thing I saw was some shiny blue cloth. I reached in and pulled it out, letting it unfold in the air in front of me.

"No. Freaking. Way," I gasped.

In my hands, was a brand new, totally authentic, Blue Jays jersey. It was a girl's version, so the sides of it were slimmed in a bit. On the back there was the number seven, Peyton Boyying's number. My favorite. There was only one person who could have sent this to me, but I glanced down at the box it came in just to check. Sure enough, Gabe's name was scribbled on the return address.

This thing must have cost at least two hundred bucks, I thought, as I slipped it on over my t-shirt.

It fit perfectly. I ran my hands over the smooth material, noticing how expensive it felt and almost feeling guilty about having it. I never splurged on anything like this and certainly wasn't used to others doing it for me. I was touched by it, though, and completely thrilled.

I know what I'm going to be wearing every single Sunday during football season from now on, I thought. *Every day forever, really.*

With my new jersey on, I made my way back upstairs to

finish the conversation with my mother. Once in my office, I sat down at my desk and picked up the cell. My smile was wider than ever as I beamed with joy from the surprise gift from Gabe.

"Hey, sorry about that, Mom."

"No problem, honey," she replied. "Who was at the door? It wasn't your new boyfriend by chance, was it?"

"No, no," I said. "Just the delivery man dropping off a package. Sorry to burst your bubble."

"What were we talking about before you answered the door?" she asked. "Oh yeah, Gabe."

"Yes, Gabe," I stated, with a dreamy smile plastered across my face.

"I can't remember the last time you went on a second date," she replied. "Do you see a future with him?"

"Mom, I've only seen him *two times*. It's impossible for me to answer that question," I said, as my smile faded with annoyance. "But I can tell you this: he's a pretty amazing guy, at least from what he's shown me so far. I mean he's taken me on two of the best dates I've ever had. He's definitely making a solid first impression."

"So you went to Dove's restaurant on your first date and then got box seats to the Blue Jays game on your second," she paused, worry coming into her voice. "I've got to ask, Harper. What does this guy do for a living?"

I rolled my eyes, as the snooping side of my mother began to be revealed. "Don't worry, Mom. He's not a mafia king," I teased her. "He's a software engineer or a computer programmer. Something like that, I don't really remember exactly, and it's not important."

"Harper, I don't think software engineers make enough money to spend a couple of thousand dollars on the first two dates with a girl. That takes serious cash, you know?

Unless he took out a loan or something to try and impress you." She let the assumption that he was bad with money just hang in the air without actually saying it. Of course the man I finally show interest in, the one that will finally get her off my back, has *something* wrong with him.

"Mom, does it really matter what he does or how he got the money?" I asked. "Shouldn't it just be enough that he took me out on some nice dates?"

"I guess you're right, Harp. It's not super important how he got the money," she replied, but without conviction. "But it is kind of important that you know what he does for a living."

"Why?" I snapped back. "*Why* does it matter?"

"Because it seems like you don't really know anything about him," she explained. "It worries me."

"That's not true, Mom. I know *plenty* about him," I replied, feeling defensive.

"Really? Like what?" she asked. "Tell me everything you know about him."

It took everything I had not to hang up my phone in frustration. I thought about her question, though, and quickly realized that she was right. I really *didn't* know very much about the guy, except that he worked with computers and appeared to have a lot of money. I didn't have a good answer for her, so I decided to just dodge the question the best I could.

"He's overall a great guy. I think that's all I need to know right now," I stated. "Can't you just be excited for me for one minute?"

"Harper, I just want you to be happy," she said. "There's no need to be short with me. I just want what's best for you."

"You want me to be happy?" I asked, feeling my blood pressure begin to rise. "I'd be a lot happier if you stopped second-guessing everything that I enjoy in life! Why can't you just stop with the questions and accept that I simply had a good night? Why do you feel like you need to plan out my entire life for me, just because I had *one* decent date. It was just a date, Mom. He's just a guy and it was just a date. Can we please leave it alone?"

I had gone from smiling with joy to yelling at my mother in less than thirty seconds.

"I'm not second-guessing anything," Mom replied, irritation and exasperation in her voice. "And I'm not planning out your life, Harper. I just want you to be happy and I don't want you to mess it up with this guy. He seems like he could be amazing and I'd hate to see you write him off as just more material for your website. I just want you to give someone a real chance, Harper. Time is flying by and you aren't getting any younger. I only want what's best for you."

I felt like banging my head against the wall. This was just a new variation on the conversation we always had. I had a feeling that even if I was dating a billionaire, Mom wouldn't think it was good enough.

"I know, Mom. I know." I sighed. "Look, can I call you a little later? I've got a lot of writing to do today and I need to get started. I'm sorry I yelled."

"It's okay, honey," she said. "Let's talk later on tonight when you're not so busy."

"Love you, Mom."

"Love you, too, Harp."

I hung up the phone and instantly felt a knot in my gut from speaking to my mother so angrily. I always felt bad when I snapped like that, but there were times when she'd just pry and pry until I couldn't take it any more.

Still, though, as mad as she made me with her constant questions about Gabe, I couldn't really deny that she had a point. I didn't know much about him and if I thought there was even a tiny possibility of this turning into a relationship, then had I better change that.

It really only left one option and that was to spend some more time talking to Gabe, which didn't sound too bad at all. I needed to thank him for my new jersey anyway, which gave me the perfect excuse to call him and set up another meeting.

CHAPTER 14

The GPS on my phone told me to take a right onto Vista Drive. I pulled over and looked at it again, just to make sure that I had typed in the address correctly. There was no way that this was the right Vista Drive.

This is weird, I thought. *There has to be something wrong.*

I had been driving for twenty minutes, following the directions to the address that Gabe had given me to come visit him at his home. My GPS had led me to the bridge that connected to one of the islands just outside of Miami, but there was no way this was the right bridge.

"This can't be right," I said, as I checked the address for the second time.

I looked out across the water to a small body of land called Virginia Key. Massive mansions decorated the top of the hills. It was by far the most prestigious area in all of Miami. This wasn't just a well-to-do part of town. The people who lived on the Virginia Key were a different kind of rich. They weren't millionaires. They were billionaires.

The thought crossed my mind that I should call up Gabe and double-check on the address, but I decided not to pursue that. Maybe he lived in one of the guest houses or something. Besides, it was just a few minutes drive to the island and even if it wasn't where Gabe lived, I figured I might as well check it out. I had lived in Miami most of my life and still hadn't gone over there to see the castles that some people referred to as "homes".

I turned onto the bridge and took the drive over the ocean. It didn't take long until I arrived at the other side. At the end of the bridge, the road ran into a giant gate, which was closed off and blocking my access. Next to the gate was a small building with a guard.

"This is ridiculous," I said to myself. "This isn't where Gabe lives. I should turn around."

It was then that I realized I *couldn't* turn around without driving up to the gate anyway, since there wasn't enough room on the two-lane road. With a sigh, I pulled up to the small building next to the gate where I was greeted by a tall man in a security uniform.

"Good afternoon, ma'am," he said through the window. "How may I help you?"

"I think I might be in the wrong place," I explained. "I'm looking for a guy named Gabe. I'm pretty sure I have the wrong address, though. Can I just turn around somewhere?"

"Gabe?" the guy asked. "Do you have a last name for him?"

I felt embarrassed, realizing that I didn't remember the last name of the guy that I was dating.

"I think it starts with an H, but I can't remember exactly," I admitted. "Honors? That sounds right. But if you can let me through the gate to turn around, I promise I won't go any further than I have to. There's just not enough room for me to flip my car around here."

"What's your name?" the guard asked. I didn't have

much of a choice, so I told him. The guy held his finger up. "Hold on one moment, ma'am. Let me just make a quick phone call."

He closed his window and I watched as he picked up the phone. Even though I hadn't done anything wrong, I somehow began to fear that the guy was calling the cops to report an intruder. I pictured myself running from the law in high heels and chuckled. After a moment, he opened his window once more.

"Okay, go ahead," he said. "Gabe confirmed your visit. Please pull through."

My eyebrows wrinkled in confusion, but I wasn't going to argue with the guy. So when the black gates lifted, I pulled my car through.

This is actually where he lives? The address was correct?

I had my hesitations, but my GPS told me to keep driving forward. According to my phone, I was still on the right path. I began to feel very out of place, though, driving my little beat up car toward the giant mansions.

"No wonder that guard didn't trust me to just turn around," I whispered, as I stared with awe at the homes in front of me. "This is probably the cheapest car that's ever driven into this neighborhood."

I only drove a half a mile, though, before I came across another gate. It was similar to the first. This time, a woman wearing the same security uniform stepped out of the building and up to my driver's side window.

"Hi there," she said, with a professional smile. "You must be Harper. May I see some ID?"

"ID?" I asked.

"It's standard protocol, ma'am." She smiled, but there was steel behind her gaze. I didn't want to mess with her.

"Um, ok," I responded, as I dug into my purse and pulled out my driver's license.

The woman took a glance at it and then swiped it through a little handheld machine, before returning it. "Have a great evening, ma'am."

She then walked back into the building and opened up the gate, allowing me in. I knew that there were gated neighborhoods, but I had no clue that there existed any that had *two* sets gates to get inside. This was insane.

Finally, though, after getting through security and steering my car along the winding road that led between the homes, I made it all the way to the back of the island. It was then that my GPS told me I had arrived at my destination. I looked up to see what I'd have called a castle. The entire house was built out of stone and it stood proudly on the edge of the surrounding golf course.

"I guess this is it," I said to myself out loud. "This is the address that Gabe gave me anyway."

I pulled into the long driveway and parked my car. Before stepping out, I quickly glanced in the rear view mirror to sure that my hair and makeup looked good.

If this is where Gabe actually lives, then he has some explaining to do about his profession. There's no way that a computer programmer could buy a place like this. No freaking way, I thought.

When I walked up to the door and knocked. I wasn't sure if knocking was appropriate for a house like this. Perhaps a gong or a rope bell. I thought for sure that I had the wrong house. Then Gabe opened the door.

"You made it," he said, with a smile. He opened the door a little wider to let me in. "You're a little early, but I'm glad you're here. I don't have dinner ready yet, just so you know."

He leaned in and gave me a peck on the lips. As he

pulled away, I accidentally gave him an obvious once over. I couldn't help it. He was wearing a light blue dress shirt and gray slacks. He looked super cute.

"I wasn't sure I would make it," I replied. "I was pretty sure that I had the wrong address."

"Yeah, people tend to think that," he said with a laugh. "Come on in."

I followed him inside and looked around, doing my best to not let my jaw hit the tile floor. The home was huge and open, by far the biggest place I had ever stepped foot in. But it was also intimate and homey at the same time. The walls were all decorated with amazing, hand-painted modern art and each room was overflowing with comfortable and expensive-looking furniture. It looked like something out of a magazine or out of as episode of MTV cribs.

"This is where you live?" I asked, as I attempted to hide my surprise. I didn't do a very good job.

"Yep, this is it," he replied. He turned and held his arms open. His eyes twinkled with enjoyment and I wondered how often he got to show his home off to surprised visitors. "Do you like it?"

How could I not? I thought. "It's really nice," I said, trying to shrug as if this were all completely normal. "How long have you lived here?"

"I bought it a couple of years ago," he said, as he led me across the main area of the home. "I used to live in down-town Miami, but I got kind of sick of the crowds. I wanted a retreat and when I saw this place, I just knew that I had to have it."

We stepped into the kitchen, which was practically the size of the first floor of my house. All of the appliances were stainless steel and the counters were made of black granite.

On the far back wall was a full-size bar, completely stocked with every kind of alcohol.

"This is amazing," I whispered. "Do you really live here?"

"This isn't even the best part," he replied. With a chuckle and a grin, he grabbed my hand and led me a little further through the house to the back patio. We stepped out to a view of the ocean that would have made a cruise ship jealous.

"Oh, my gosh. This is absolutely insane," I whispered.

The guy owned a mansion with an ocean view. I couldn't help but to be impressed, but also a little curious. I found myself wondering just how much money he had. What exactly did he do that gave him a house like this? Did he belong to a rich family maybe? Won the lottery?

It's none of your business, Harper. It doesn't matter how much he has, I told myself.

If I was going to be with Gabe, I wanted to be with him because he was a great guy, not because he has an amazing house with a lot of money. Though, I had to admit that those things definitely didn't hurt.

I stepped up to the railing overlooking the view and Gabe came up next to me, placing a hand on my lower back. A small thrill went through me and my heart fluttered at his touch.

"It's beautiful, isn't it?" he asked. "This view is the biggest reason I wanted this place."

"I love the ocean," I said, taking in a deep breath of salty air.

"Me too. I love it, because it's a constant reminder of just how small we are in comparison to the world," he said softly. "It's humbling. It's honest and real."

I turned to face him. The setting sun fell across his face,

lighting up his eyes and accentuating his gorgeous features. Not only was Gabe absolutely beautiful but it was becoming clear that he was also extremely deep and intelligent.

"That was poetic," I responded. "Did you write that yourself?"

"No, but I have more." He laughed and then put on his best serious expression again. "I'm small compared to the world. It's just a fact. I just like to remind myself of it so that I can stay humble. Everyone can use more humility."

I couldn't help but laugh. He joined in, his laugh complimenting mine and making me feel comfortable standing there.

We had our arms wrapped around each other for a moment, just taking in the view. Standing there next to him, I realized that there really wasn't any place I'd rather be. But a moment later, the peace was shattered by a crashing sound coming from the kitchen. We both turned around immediately in surprise.

"What in the hell was that?" I asked, suddenly a little spooked. Apparently this house was either haunted or we weren't alone.

"Sorry. Dropped a pan. I just brought in all of the dinner ingredients, Gabe." A man wearing a long-sleeved t-shirt poked his head out of the patio door. "And, she's already here. Everything you need is on the counter."

"Hey, Bastian," Gabe said, as he led me across the patio. "This is Harper."

The man came out to greet me, holding out his hand. The motion was reluctant. He was a good looking guy, though there was a faint scar running from his cheek to his eyebrow. His short, golden-brown hair was neatly groomed, which contrasted Gabe's messy look.

"I'm not actually supposed to be here," he said. Gabe

glared at him, so he smiled politely. "It's nice to meet you. How are you?"

"I'm well," I responded, not quite sure what to make of him. Where Gabe was easy going, this man was brooding and intense.

"Harper, this is my best friend, Bastian," Gabe jumped in. "I've known him forever. Sometimes he also helps me out around here, since I need all the help I can get."

"Seriously, you do," Bastian joked back, losing some of his intensity and opening up. "I don't know what you would do without my help, honestly. This place would fall apart or you'd starve to death, and I'm not sure which would happen first."

I giggled softly. "Did you say you brought dinner ingredients?"

"I did," he said. His eyes were incredibly light and full of confidence and power. "Gabe said he wanted to make a special dinner, but he didn't have time to get the food. I offered to help him out."

"That's really sweet of you," I said. The dark aura he projected didn't quite fit with him bringing Gabe dinner. I wondered for a moment if he was in the Mob and that was how Gabe was making his money.

"Yeah, well, Gabe would do the same for me," he said. "Right, Gabe?"

"Of course," Gabe said, leading us back inside. "You're practically my brother."

I watched as Gabe walked over to the kitchen counter and pulled steaks out of the reusable grocery bag while Bastian helped.

"Are you going to make me dinner?" I asked, with a smile that showed my surprise.

"I wanted to try," he explained. Bastian snorted and

Gabe glared at him before turning to me with a defeated sigh. "I'll be completely honest with you, though. I'm probably the worst cook of all time."

Bastian jumped in on the conversation. "He's not lying, Harper. The guy can't even seem to make Ramen noodles without screwing it up."

"Bastian, everybody knows that I make the best Ramen noodles in town," Gabe shot back. He winked at me and made a face at Bastian. Bastian just rolled his eyes at Gabe and kept unloading the ingredients.

"Only eat his meal if you are an exceptional actress," Bastian advised. "I was supposed to come and cook it all for him, so then he could claim it as his own after I left."

"Way to rat me out, Bro." Gabe glared at Bastian a little harder. Bastian just shrugged and kept setting things on the counter.

"I think it's sweet that you wanted to try to make me dinner," I said, leaning against the counter. "Even if you weren't going to do it yourself. I'd still eat whatever you made, though, Gabe."

Bastian paused and looked over at Gabe. "You like her, so I'm going to cook so you don't kill her with food poisoning."

"I'm not that bad," Gabe protested.

Bastian turned toward me. "He is that bad. One time, he got our entire house sick. And we only had one bathroom. Let me tell you, it was terrible. And all his fault."

"Thank you for that, Bastian." Gabe massaged the bridge of his nose and made a face. "I may kill you. And not just with food poisoning. I'm still semi-trying to impress her."

"Don't worry, you already impressed me," I assured him. I came over and kissed his cheek. "But, I would probably prefer it if you didn't cook."

Bastian looked over at Gabe and started to laugh, finally losing the dark look about him. When he smiled, the scar lessened. He wasn't nearly as intimidating.

"I'll cook the food while you guys relax. Then we can all eat together since Ava's out of town tonight. How does that sound?" Bastian offered. "That way no one will die of food poisoning and I get to eat."

"Do you need any help?" I asked.

"I very much appreciate the offer, but I've got it handled." Bastian maneuvered around the kitchen, throwing the steaks into a sizzling pan and steaming vegetables at the same time. "Why don't you two go relax in the dining room and I'll be in with the food in just a few minutes."

"Thanks, buddy," Gabe said.

We walked over to a comfortable living room and sat down next to each other on a couch. Again the artwork was modern and beautiful, but it didn't tell me much about the man I was sitting next to. I could hear Bastian moving around the kitchen and things were starting to smell delicious. My mouth was already watering.

"So tell me more about Bastian. You said that you guys are best friends," I said, snuggling into Gabe's shoulder. I figured that if I knew more about his best friend, I would know more about Gabe.

"We're practically family. He and I met when we were young," Gabe explained, wrapping his arm around me. "Bastian had a rough childhood, so he spent most of it at my house. We've gone through everything together and he's always had my back no matter what."

I instantly thought of Cora. The relationship sounded pretty similar.

"He sounds like a great guy," I said. I put my head on

Gabe's shoulder, loving the way he felt strong and warm underneath me.

"He's the best," Gabe agreed. "A bit of jerk, but still the best."

I chuckled. "Tell me something I don't know about you."

"Hmmm, well, I'm horrible at golf and yet I live on a golf course," he offered. "That sums me up pretty well."

I laughed and then playfully pressed his shoulder. "I'm being serious. I don't know much about you. You said you do computer programming, right?"

"Software engineering and internet marketing," he said. He squeezed my shoulder and smiled. "It's a bunch of boring nerdy stuff, remember?"

"Yeah, but I want to know about it," I pried, about to start asking more questions until I realized I was starting to sound like my mother. "You don't have to go into detail if you don't want to, though."

"I just don't think you'd really be interested in the details," he said with a shrug. "Because honestly, it's super boring stuff. Think about numbers and spreadsheets and profit margins and that about sums it up."

It seemed that was about the best I was going to get out of him regarding his job and I didn't feel comfortable enough to just right out and ask him. If I did, I'd have just straight up inquired how he made enough money to afford a house like this. Luckily, I wasn't *that* much like my mother.

"Fair enough," I said. I changed the subject back to Bastian. "Who's Ava?"

"Bastian's wife," Gabe replied. "If you think he's broody and hard to get along with now, you should have seen him before he met her. She's practically turned him into Mr. Sunshine."

Right then, Bastian stepped around the corner, holding some plates of steaming food. "Dinner's ready."

Gabe unwrapped his arm from my shoulder and then helped me stand. Together we walked back to the kitchen table and sat down.

"I hope you were talking about me," Bastian said as he set the plates down in front of us.

"We definitely were," Gabe said. He turned and fake whispered into my ear: "Don't tell him what I said."

Bastian rolled his eyes at Gabe. "See if I cook for you again."

"This looks amazing, Bastian," I commented, as my mouth began to water. The steaks smelled incredible and I couldn't wait to dig in. There was a filet mignon, steamed local veggies, and some sort of risotto that looked good enough to be in a restaurant.

"Hopefully it tastes as good as it looks," Bastian said. "I'm trying a new recipe and I'm not sure it's perfected yet."

We sat down to eat, and Bastian continued. "So tell me about yourself, Harper. What do you do for work?"

"I'm a freelance writer," I explained. A small twinge of guilt passed through me. I knew I was going to have to come clean to Gabe eventually about what I did, but I wasn't ready to tell him yet. And I certainly wasn't ready to tell his best friend.

"Really? What do you write about?" Bastian smiled, but it didn't quite touch his eyes. For a moment, I wondered if he knew what I really did.

Don't be silly, Harper, I chided myself. *If he did, he would have told Gabe by now and you wouldn't be sitting here.*

"I do a fair amount of magazine articles, but I'll pretty much write anything," I replied, choosing my words carefully. "Writing is my only income, so I have to do what it takes, you know?"

"Of course," Bastian agreed. "That makes sense to me. And Gabe mentioned that you two met online, is that right?"

"We did!" I replied. I felt better talking about this part. There was no subterfuge here. "We met on Kindling Dating and I have to say that he has surprised me in every way. My online dating experiences had been pretty awful until I met Gabe."

"I hear Kindling Dating is the best," Bastian said, taking another bite.

Gabe shot Bastian a look I couldn't decipher and then wrapped an arm around me. He leaned in to kiss my cheek. "That's what I've been told," Gabe said. "Numerous times."

Bastian smiled and this time it was real. "Well, I'm glad you guys found each other. I can't deny that you make a cute couple."

"Thanks," I said. "I'm pretty happy he knows someone who can cook. This is delicious!"

The topics went to the weather and the latest Blue Jays game. Bastian wasn't as big of a fan as Gabe, but he was able to hold his own in conversation. We ate dinner and the whole time I sat with my chair scooted up next to Gabe's. We were practically cuddling as we ate, unable to stay away from each other. Bastian laughed at our shameless displays of affection, but I didn't mind. I hadn't been with a guy that I wanted to act like that with in too long to remember.

I liked Bastian. The longer he talked, the more I warmed up to him. He seemed like a great guy and a really good friend to Gabe. But I couldn't help but feel an undercurrent of *"are you good enough for my friend?"* It was odd and I was unable to pin it down exactly. I eventually just chalked it up as normal, figuring that Cora would do the same thing to Gabe once she got to meet him.

After we finished our meals, Bastian stood up from his chair and cleared our plates. "Alright guys, I've got to get back home."

"You're leaving already?" I asked.

"Seriously, Bastian, you just got here," Gabe chimed in. "Have a drink with us."

"I'm afraid that if I watch you two kids loving all over each other any longer, I just might throw up the delicious meal I just ate," Bastian joked. "So, thanks, but no thanks."

Gabe responded, "Hey, how long have I been putting up with you and Ava making out in front of me while I tried to have a conversation?"

Bastian nodded. "Good point. But I still don't care."

Gabe laughed and Bastian grinned at him good-naturedly. "Thanks again for making dinner, Bastian," Gabe told him.

"Yes, thank you, Bastian," I chimed in. "The food was incredible."

"You're quite welcome," he said. "It was great to meet you, Harper. I love seeing Gabe this happy."

Before I could come up with a reply, he nodded to both of us and walked out the front door, leaving Gabe and I alone.

"I'm sorry if he came across as a little..." Gabe paused to think of the word. "Protective? Intimidating?"

"Protective is a good word," I agreed. "I think he really cares about you. But I think he warmed up to me."

"I do too," Gabe said with a nod. "I'm glad he didn't scare you away. He can be a bit much."

I looked out from one of the big windows overlooking the water. The sun was finally setting and from where we sat, I could see the sky outside as it began to turn orange. It looked to be a breathtaking sunset.

"Can we watch the sunset?" I asked, already standing up.

"Of course!" Gabe said, nearly knocking over his chair and taking my hand.

I followed him out to the patio and we stepped up to the railing. The ocean sprawled out in front of us, all the way to the horizon, where the sun sat lonely on the water. The sky was on fire, making the incredible view from the island even more breathtaking. A warm breeze blew off of the sea, causing my hair to fall across my forehead. Gabe reached over and pushed the loose hair over my ear. His touch was soft, as if he were afraid I might disappear if he touched me.

"You look beautiful tonight," he said. "Thank you for coming over for dinner."

I smiled as I stepped closer to him. "The food was wonderful. But I'm still pretty excited to try out your world famous Ramen noodles one of these days."

Gabe chuckled and then leaned in, surprising me with a kiss. The passion in the air ignited instantly as we embraced in front of the sunset. The island air blew through my hair, carrying with it the scent of saltwater and warm sand. It was a picture perfect moment; one that I never saw myself actually experiencing. This island kiss was the most romantic kiss of my life.

Gabe gently pulled away, just long enough to look at me with those glowing green eyes. Then he leaned in again. Our lips parted this time and the kiss became more passionate, with our tongues delicately dancing. My hands drifted up his back. I could feel the definition of his muscles, even over his shirt, and it turned me on even more. I wanted to feel his naked skin, his firm body, all of him and all at once.

This is what I've wanted for so long, I thought. *And I want so much more.*

It was as though he had heard my thoughts. Gabe slowly broke our kiss and then brought his lips to the outside of my neck. My jaw dropped and I let out a silent gasp as he kissed my sensitive skin, inching his way down toward my shoulder. My body was on fire now and a desperate aching presented itself in my most sensitive areas.

Gabe pulled away and looked at me. His eyes had dilated and there was an expression of animalistic lust on his face. He was breathing harder than before and when I glanced down, I noticed a growing bulge in the front of his slacks. No words were exchanged. There were none needed.

Everything that could have been said was written all over our faces and our body language. We wanted each other right then and there, and all of the time we had spent together so far had just been leading up to this magical moment.

"Kiss me," I whispered.

He did as I asked and brought his lips to mine once again. Sweet and hot, our tongues tangled together. Our inhibitions quickly faded, replaced by a relentless passion. It was almost as if I had lost control, submitting to my most carnal desires.

My hands drifted over his body. I loved the way his muscular shoulders flexed with even the tiniest of his movements. I couldn't get enough of his biceps either, which swelled as he pulled me close. Everything about this man turned me on.

After a moment, Gabe broke our kiss and then grabbed

my hand, leading me across the porch to a lounging area that had a circle of padded patio furniture on it. In front of us, the sky had turned from orange into a shade of deep purple as the sun continued its decline behind the horizon. The stars were beginning to show and the night air cooled, though it was still comfortably warm.

"You're something else, Harper," Gabe commented. His eyes pupils dilated as he looked me over. "I can't put my finger on it, but there's something about you that drives me crazy. And I mean that in the best of ways."

I simply smiled coyly as I sat down on one of lounge chairs and patted the seat next to me. The bulge in Gabe's pants had grown significantly and was pushing out against the material. He wanted me. Just seeing that turned me on even more and caused the desperate aching inside of me to increase. I wanted what was underneath that cloth. I wanted it so badly.

Gabe crawled onto the padded lounger with me, pushing my shoulder with one hand and cradling my head with the other as he lay me down. He nipped at my exposed collarbone, dragging his teeth along the soft flesh and making me gasp with desire. The bottom of my dress shifted upwards as I wrapped my legs around him. It felt strange to be so exposed outside, but given that there was nothing but ocean in front of us, I wasn't worried about being seen.

Gabe paused in his kisses, pulling back for a moment and looking me over. His pupils dilated further. "You are so gorgeous," he whispered reverently.

I couldn't help but to blush at the compliment. I had been called gorgeous before, but when Gabe said it, it just *felt* different. There was such sincerity in him. It wasn't just in his voice, though. It was written all over his face too. He looked at me like he *needed* me in that moment and it made my insides turn to butterflies. All girls have their insecurities and I was no different, but when Gabe complimented me, it was like all of those things faded away. He truly made me feel beautiful.

After a second of admiring me, Gabe leaned in and kissed the top of my bare shoulder, causing pleasurable little goose bumps to pop up on my skin. I wrapped my legs around his waist and pulled him closer, feeling as his bulge pressed against the front of my panties. The friction sent of burst of pleasure into me and I moaned softly. The desperate craving inside of me begged for him, all of him.

"Gabe," I whispered, more to release the pressure building inside of me than to get his attention.

I wanted to tell him to take me right there, but I couldn't even get the words out. He had begun to grind his hips forward, increasing the friction and intensifying the pleasure.

Gabe moved his face downward toward my chest and kissed the top of my cleavage, letting out a lustful growl. My lips parted and I breathed in, pushing my chest upward and against his face. His skin was smooth with only a hint of stubble and I knew he must have shaved before I came over. My dress allowed him access to only a little bit of my cleavage, but I wanted him to have it all. I wanted his kiss all over my body.

"Let me take this off," I said, propping myself up on my elbows.

He held himself over me and then sat back. I quickly pulled the dress over my head, before tossing it onto a nearby lounge chair. Then I relaxed back into the cushion, sprawled in front of him in nothing but my bra and panties.

"Your turn," I ordered, with a sexual smile.

"I like when you tell me what you want," he replied, his

mouth turning into a cocky smile. Gabe quickly unbuttoned his dress shirt. I watched as his chiseled chest and washboard abs were revealed.

You've got to be kidding me, I thought. *He's absolutely perfect. Better than perfect.*

He tossed the shirt to the side and the reached down to take off his belt. His muscles flexed as he moved and my jaw continued to drop. He was absolutely gorgeous. His skin was tan and his body was ripped. He looked more like an underwear model than he did a software engineer. While he took off his pants, I reached down and gently pinched the top of my thigh, just to make sure that I wasn't dreaming.

It turned out that I wasn't.

Gabe stripped down all the way to his gray boxer briefs. He stood there at the foot of the lounge chair and I took in the view.

With my index finger, I used the "come hither" motion to get him back over. He obliged and resumed his position, hovering over me. Now that my dress was off, he had full access to my cleavage and he didn't hesitate to bring his mouth there, gently biting and kissing my sensitive skin.

Our bodies became entwined. I wrapped my legs around him and pulled him close, once again feeling the friction, though now there was even less cloth between us. My senses lit up and waves of pleasure pumped into me with each movement of our hips. While Gabe kissed my cleavage, I unclasped the front of my bra to fully release my breasts. He let out a sexual growl and then brought his mouth over one of my nipples.

I gasped as his flicked his tongue against the sensitive bud, causing it to grow firm in an instant.

"Yes..." I panted.

Gabe gently licked and nibbled on the top of my breasts,

creating a combination of pain and pleasure that had my senses exploding. He focused on that for a moment and then brought his face to the other side of my chest to give equal attention to my other breast. I was in heaven. Total heaven. There was nothing else I wanted in the entire world in that moment, except for more of what Gabe was already giving me.

His hands slid up my naked front. He gently fondled my breasts while continuing to use his mouth in the most miraculous way. His tongue and mouth were lethal weapons that threatened to destroy me completely. I became wet with eagerness. I couldn't wait for him to pleasure the rest of my body.

While he focused on my chest, I slipped off my panties, letting them fall to the ground next to the chair. Gabe pulled away and gave me a slow once over. Then he brought his face to my belly, inching his way downward toward my most sensitive area. I lifted my legs and placed them over his shoulders, positioning myself so that his face was right between my legs.

"Perfect." The word escaped his lips as if he didn't even realize he had said it.

A moment later, I felt the slight stubble on his cheeks scratch the inside of my thighs as he leaned in and began to devour me sexually. I let out a squeal of bliss, as his tongue pressed against my flower, creating a powerful rush of ecstasy.

I groaned, arching my back and writhing on the lounge. My body twisted to give him better access, and my hands tangled in his dark hair.

Gabe continued to ravage me, kissing and tonguing me in a way I didn't even know a person could do. He moved his face down and then back up, giving extra attention to the most sensitive parts. Electricity zapped and flowed through my spine, overwhelming my system completely.

"Gabe," I gasped as my mind turned to a kaleidoscope of pleasure and color.

Gabe continued to pleasure me for another moment until my body stopped shaking, and then slowly pulled away. He stood up and slipped off his underwear.

He looks better naked than he does with clothes on, I thought. *How is that even possible?*

With ease, Gabe lifted me up, placing one arm under my knees and the other across my back. I wrapped an arm around the back of his neck and held on as he walked me across the porch and back into the house. We made our way upstairs to the master bedroom, where he laid me down on his King-sized bed.

I watched as he grabbed a condom out of his dresser and slipped it on as he made his way back to the bed. It made me happy that he only wanted to have sex with me the safe way. It said good things about him.

"Come here," I whispered, as I grabbed his hands and gently pulled him onto the bed with me.

"Now where were we?" Gabe mused. He grinned, his smile lighting up the room and speeding up my heart. He grabbed my legs and pulled me to him as he stood by the side of the bed.

I wrapped my legs around his waist. His erect cock hovered just in front of my opening. He bucked his hips forward a tiny bit, pressing just inside of me, but not fully.

"God, yes," I whispered. "Yes."

With my legs, I pulled him toward me even further, easing him in. I drew in a quick breath through my teeth as sensation filled me from head to toe. The desperate aching turned into a tremble of pleasure, as Gabe began to rock his hips, slipping in a little further with each movement.

My eyes rolled into my head and my back arched. I reached to my sides, gripping the blanket below me with both hands. The soft cotton material clenched in my grip as I held on, using it to stay put against Gabe's movement.

"That feels amazing," I said, though my words trailed off at the end.

Gabe let out a soft grunt as he slid the rest of the way in. I closed my eyes, focusing on the tightening of my body against his. He began to rock his body quickly against mine, sending waves of ecstasy into me with each plunge.

When I opened my eyes, I saw a view that was even more incredible than the sunset off of Gabe's deck. His muscular body, his tanned skin, the look of lust in his eyes, the way his dark hair fell across his forehead. It was a fantasy come to life.

Gabe leaned forward and kissed my neck. I breathed him in, enjoying his intoxicating scent. It was a combination of his natural musk and the expensive cologne that he always wore. I breathed him in, taking him into me in every way possible.

Each of his thrusts filled me with another surge of bliss, overwhelming me with sensation. Every inch of my body cried out in ecstasy as our bodies continue to collide. The pleasure intensified as he increased his pace, causing me to climb toward orgasm yet again.

My eyes closed once more and my back arched high as I climaxed. I rode the wave of ecstasy as far as it would take me, letting it flow through my entire body. When it was over, I relaxed back down onto the soft blanket. It took a moment for me to regain my senses. This one was far more powerful than the first. I hadn't had an intense orgasm like that in some time and when I finally opened my eyes, I noticed that my hands and legs were trembling from it.

Moonlight had begun to pour in through the bedroom window. The light blanketed over us, causing the definition in Gabe's muscles to become more apparent. I brought my hands to his forearms, letting my fingers slide upward toward his shoulders.

We made love like this for a while, before he finally slowed down. He was breathing hard, causing his chest to rise and fall in cadence. He kissed me again and then rolled onto his back and up onto the bed. I knew exactly what he wanted. He didn't even have to ask.

I crawled over the top of him, straddling his lap. His cock was erect between my legs, as I hovered a few inches above it. Gabe reached up and placed his hands onto my breasts, drawing my nipples between his fingers and sending a pleasurable chill through me. At the same time, I slowly dropped my weight downward, letting his thickness enter me once more.

"Oh, God yes," Gabe whispered. His eyes rolled back into his head and I watched his adam's apple bob as he swallowed hard.

Slowly at first, I rode him. It felt good to be the one in control. I watched Gabe's face change from relaxed into intense concentration as I quickened my pace a little bit. His eyes closed and his lush lips parted.

"Like this?" I asked. I wanted to make sure that he was enjoying this as much as I was.

He didn't even say anything in response. He just gave a quick nod, as the side of his lips began to curl into a pleasurable grimace. Clearly, I was moving the way he liked. His expression said it all. So I increased my pace a little further, bouncing up and down on his lap in a rhythmic dance that consumed me with pleasure.

"Just like that," Gabe finally said, his voice tight and husky with desire.

His hands slid along my thighs, landing on my backside. He held me like that, bucking his hips upward and holding himself in me. An animalist grunt escaped his lips and a moment later, I felt his cock swell inside of me.

He groaned, low and deep. It vibrated through my entire being as he lost himself to me. His fingers gripped my ass and his hips shuddered as he found release. Heat and desire washed over me, and I cried out, a high pitched scream to counter his low growl.

I slowed my movement down to a stop, then finally caught my breath. Gabe slowly opened his eyes. He looked so relaxed and content after having climaxed.

"You're amazing," he said, before sitting up and giving me a sensual kiss on the lips.

"You're not too bad yourself," I teased, pushing a strand of hair out of my face. He reached up and pushed another from my forehead before leaning forward and kissing me again.

His lips were soft and his arms strong as he pulled me to him. Our skin touched at every available spot and for the first time in a long time, I could say I was truly happy.

LATER THAT EVENING, I opened my eyes and looked around. It was just past midnight, but I found myself awake for no good reason. The bed was perfectly soft, the sheets were comfortable, I wasn't too hot or too cold- but I couldn't sleep. Gabe, however, was still sound asleep in the bed next to me.

I watched him for a moment. His chest rose and fell smoothly and his dark lashes stayed closed. He smiled softly in his sleep and murmured my name. He looked so peaceful and content, that I didn't want to wake him.

I closed my eyes for a bit, trying to fall back into my peaceful slumber, but I just couldn't. I had a burst of energy and it was clear that sleep wouldn't be coming back any time soon. So I hopped out of bed and got dressed. I grabbed my laptop from my car, bringing it back to the huge leather couch in Gabe's living room.

I might as well do some work if I'm not going to sleep tonight, I thought.

Within a few seconds, I had my website pulled up. I hadn't made a personal blog post in a while and it was clear that I'd lost some of my traffic because of it. My readers wanted new content every single day and if they didn't get it, then I knew they wouldn't stick around for long.

Up to this point, I had limited my blog posts to be about bad dates involving friends, family or personal experience; basically anything that I could verify to some degree. But without me having regular bad dates, I just didn't have the content I needed to keep the website running smoothly. I needed more.

That was when an idea flashed into my mind.

What if I allowed readers to submit their stories to me? They could tell me all about their bad dates and I could post the best "worst" dates from them. It'll be like a contest.

My eyes lit up as I typed furiously on my computer, writing up a blog post that asked for reader's submissions. I decided to call it "Worst Wednesday". Every week, I'd decide which of my readers had had the worst date and then I'd publish it.

It was a decent stop-gap, but I knew it wouldn't take the place of my regular posts. I needed something else.

I looked around Gabe's living room, taking in my surroundings for a moment. I thought about Gabe and how much I was really starting to like him. Like really *like* him, not just pure physical attraction. The physical attraction was definitely there, but I actually liked spending time with him. It wasn't just purely sexual, it was mental too. My time with him always felt well spent and there was really nobody else I wanted to date because of it.

My fingers hovered over the keyboard. If I didn't go on dates, then I wouldn't have anything to blog about. I couldn't do that or I'd starve. My blog was how I paid my bills. There was really only one option.

So, with some hesitation, I decided that I'd start blogging about my good dates with him. Every other day, except Worst Wednesday, I'd post about what I did with Gabe. With any luck, they'd fall in love with him too.

I'm over trying to hide this from the world, I thought.

With that, I got busy writing my second post of the night. In it, I told all about how much I'd been spoiled over the past couple of dates with Gabe and how it was nearly impossible for me to think of anything bad to say about him.

At the time, I had no clue how the readers were going to react. I never could have guessed how some in particular reacted.

CHAPTER 15

I couldn't remember the last time I had been this happy. It felt like I had been walking on a cloud and even two days after Gabe and I hooked up, there was still a smile on my face. Everything with him was going so well. He was exactly the type of gentleman I had always imagined, though never actually believed I could end up with.

It wasn't just Gabe that had me smiling, though. It was also my website and blog. My latest post about the amazing dates with Gabe had had a really good response, much better than I imagined they would. In fact, I was getting emails daily from readers, asking me if Gabe was real or just a made up person.

The next Tuesday afternoon, I was sitting in my computer chair just casually looking at the comments on my blog, when I got a phone call from Cora. I hadn't talked to her in a couple of days, so I jumped at the opportunity and answered the call.

"Cora! How are you?" I asked, closing my browser to give her my full attention.

"Fantastic," she replied. "Although, it doesn't sound like I'm doing quite as well as you."

"What do you mean?"

"You know that I'm your biggest fan, Harper. I read your blog more regularly than anyone," she replied. "I've been learning all about Mr. Perfect Match from your website."

Guilt hit me hard. I slumped in my chair and wished I could go back in time to make just one phone call to my friend.

"I'm sorry you had to find out about him through the blog, Cora," I explained. "I've just been busy and there aren't enough minutes in the day."

"I understand. I'm just giving you a hard time," she said, her voice shifting from disappointed to cheerful. "But now that we're talking, you need to tell me all about him. Or at the very least, tell me when I can meet the guy."

"I think you'll meet him at some point. But it's still too soon for me to say for sure whether or not this is the real deal," I told her. I started to spin my chair in slow, lazy circles. "I mean Gabe is a great guy, an *amazing* guy, actually, but I still don't know where it's headed. I'm scared that I'll jinx it if I get my hopes up."

"Harper, you met his best friend the other day, right?" Cora giggled on the other end of the line. Her high-pitched, squeaky laugh always caused me to smile. "That's what you said on one of the blog posts. Something about his friend, Bastian, making you two dinner at his house?"

"Yeah, that happened." I shrugged. "But I'm not sure what that has to do with anything."

"You met his best friend, Harp! It means *everything*! If a guy introduces you to his best friend, then that means he's super into you." She had to be shaking her head at me. "It's as big of a deal as meeting his mother."

"Really? I guess I hadn't thought about that." I stopped spinning for a moment.

"It's true," she went on. "It means your relationship is probably more serious than you think."

I smiled at the thought of a serious relationship with Gabe. I actually really liked the idea of that.

"We'll see how things turn out," I replied, starting my spin back up again. "I'm not getting my hopes up quite yet, though. A part of me is still expecting it to fall apart. I guess that's what I'm used to, so I'm worried it's going to happen any minute."

"Based on what I've read about the time you've spent with him, you've got nothing to worry about, Harper," she assured me. "Gabe sounds like a wonderful guy. I doubt things will fall apart between you two."

"I hope you're right," I replied.

"So when do I get to meet him?" Cora asked again.

"If things keep going like they're going now, then we'll make plans for you to meet him in the next few weeks. How does that sound?" I asked, picking up a pencil and playing with it while I spun around in my chair.

"It sounds like a maybe, and maybe usually means no," Cora stated. I could tell she was pouting, just by the sound of her voice.

"No, it's just later," I corrected her. I decided to change the subject. "Cora, let's talk about something else. I haven't had a chance to catch up with you in a long time. How are things going for you? Any bad dates?"

"I've had a few interesting ones," she said, her voice changing back to its peppy self. "A guy who was obsessed with his handlebar mustache, a thirty-five year old who still lived with his mother, and one dude that apparently had sixteen different pets."

"Whoa." I was impressed. Cora had about the same dating track record I did, but she said she wasn't a good enough writer to do a blog of hers. She occasionally would write one up for me, and the results were always good.

"Yeah, tell me about it," she replied. "It's been a weird couple of weeks for me in the dating scene."

"Are you still willing to write about them?" I asked. "The blog has been doing well, but I think there are still plenty of readers who'd prefer to hear about bad dates over my good ones."

"I'm happy to write up some posts for you, Harper," she said. I could hear voices in the background like she was at a cafe. "But I don't know how many I'll actually have. I might be able to do one post per week or something."

Her response reminded me about the reader submission idea I had been working on.

"Did you see Sunday's post?" I asked. "The one about having readers submit their worst date stories to me? What do you think about that?"

"I *did* see that. At first, I didn't like the idea. The blog was originally about you and that's what people wanted to hear about," she said slowly. "But then I know my posts do okay."

"They do way better than 'okay'" I retorted. "Your post about the guy who was obsessed with yarn is still one of the top ten."

"That's my point. The more I thought about it, the more I realized that it's actually a great idea," she explained. "I'll bet every single girl out there has a nightmare date story they'd love to tell about and have published to your website. I think it would give the blog a little more flavor, since you'd have stories from all different women, from all over the world."

"I'm glad you liked the idea," I said, with a pleased smile.

I felt a tightness in my shoulders loosen that I hadn't realized was there. "I haven't had any submissions from it yet, but I'm thinking that I probably will. It's only been a couple of days, so I should try to be patient."

"I'm positive people will send you some stories," Cora said. "Will you forward me the juicy ones, even if you don't publish them to the site?"

"Of course!" I replied. "I have a feeling there will be some good ones that we can laugh about."

"I'll get my 'handle bar mustache man' story written up and emailed to you by this evening," she promised.

"Perfect!" I said. "And since you'll be the first one, then you'll also probably be the winner of 'Worst Wednesday', so I'll make sure it gets posted by tomorrow."

Cora cleared her throat. She didn't say anything for a moment and I knew she was thinking about something.

"So, Harper," she finally said.

"What is it, Cora?"

"I *seriously* want to meet this Gabe guy." She was using her serious voice. "Like tomorrow. I'll fly out there tomorrow."

I couldn't help but to burst out laughing. Typical Cora. She was going to bug me about meeting Gabe until it happened and there wasn't a thing I could do about it.

"You crack me up," I said. "I told you that if things worked out with him then you could meet him in a few weeks."

"Not good enough," she scolded. "You and I both know that things *are* going to work out with the relationship, so I want to set an actual date for us all to get together."

"Co-ra..." I said, exaggerating each syllable.

"Har-per..." she mimicked. "It's only fair. I think you can give me this much. I mean after all, I *did* have to learn about

Gabe from the blog. How about a friend-date? I can fly out to Orlando and we can all go out to eat."

A sigh escaped my lips. "I don't know... Like I said, I'm just afraid that if I get my hopes up about Gabe, then something will happen to keep things from working out between us. I guess I'm just being superstitious."

"Superstitious or not, I want this friend date," Cora replied. "If I don't get to meet this guy soon, then I'm going to get onto Kindling Dating and set up my *own* profile so that I can make it happen myself!"

She was making it sound like she was just joking with her threat, but I also knew her well enough to not trust that. If Cora wanted something, she'd get it. That was one thing we definitely had in common.

"You'd make your own profile just to meet Gabe?" I asked.

"I don't know if I'd get to meet him, but I'd at least have the chance to learn about him based one what he's written in his profile."

She's not going to budge on this, is she? I thought to myself.

"I love you, Cora. But you're crazy, you know that?" I mused.

"Oh, I know," she said, with a chuckle. "But I'll take it one step further. If you don't set a date for me to meet Mr. Perfect Match, then I won't send you my bad date stories for the blog."

"You're serious?" I asked. "But you promised to help me out!"

"Completely serious," she said. "This is how bad I want to meet him."

"Gabe is just some guy I'm dating, though," I explained. "I don't see why it's such a huge deal."

"No, Harper. No. He's not just *some* guy. He's the *only* guy you've dated in the past however many years who isn't a total loser. He's the opposite of every guy you've been with," she informed me. "This isn't just *some* guy! He's practically a legend, at least until I can see him in person and verify that he's actually real."

I shrugged. There was no arguing with her.

"Okay, Cora," I said. "You drive a hard bargain, but you've made yourself a deal. How about the first weekend of next month you can meet Gabe? Does that work?"

"Yes!" she squealed. "That works perfectly. I'll plan on driving down, so I'll be there that Friday evening."

While Cora was celebrating her victory, I started to think more about her idle threat to make a profile so that she could learn about Gabe. It gave me an idea.

"Cora, I know you were kind of joking about making a dating profile on Kindling Dating, but would you consider actually doing it?"

"I was only *half* joking about that," she corrected. "But yes, I suppose I could make a dating profile. Why?"

"Tell you what," I said. "Let *me* make the profile for you. I want to check out the sign up process for the website. I didn't get a chance to do that, since Rosie secretly made mine. But once I have it made, then you could use it to set up your own awful dates. Or possible really great dates."

"Hmmm," Cora responded. "I suppose I'm okay with that. But do you think I'd be able to get any awful dates from the website?"

"If there are any more self-centered men with handlebar mustaches still left in the world, Cora, then they'll find you on any dating site. Trust me."

"Okay, then sure!" she said. "Make a profile for me! This actually sounds like it could be fun."

WE CHIT-CHATTED FOR A LITTLE LONGER, going over some of the details about her upcoming trip to visit me in Orlando before hanging up.

I hung up the phone excited for what was going to happen next. The very first thing I did was to pull up the Kindling Dating site and begin the process of creating Cora's profile.

After filling in her basic information, like a profile name, email address and photo, I was asked to fill out a fifty-question survey to see what kind of mate would best suit her. I was rather impressed that Rosie had filled this out for me.

I did the best I could, answering the questions in a way that I imagined Cora would. But I couldn't help but wonder just how my answers would affect whatever algorithms Kindling Dating used to match people up. It made me ponder how Rosie might have answered these same questions for me, and if those responses could have had an effect on why I had been matched with Gabe.

Somewhere in the back of my mind, I wondered if Gabe was just dating the version Rosie had supplied or if he was actually interested in me.

CHAPTER 16

"Here, Harper, use this brush to cut in the paint next to the ceiling," Mom told me, holding out a brush. "It's angled so that you can get it perfect."

"Nobody is going to ever look up here," I said, as I took the brush from her.

"Your nephew will be looking up there every day from the crib," Mom said. "So we have to make it look as good as possible."

"Because everybody knows that all newborn babies critique the paint jobs of their nurseries," I joked.

"Harper, please," Rosie piped in, as she stepped into the room with us. "Just do what Mom says. She wants the room to be perfect, just like her new grandbaby will be."

"I was just joking around," I murmured, before dipping the little brush into the green paint.

"Why did you go with the color green, anyway, Rosie?" I asked.

"Because green is considered a calming color," Rosie explained. "I thought it would be good since he's going to have to put up with the two of you."

"That's actually pretty smart," I said, carefully pressing the paintbrush to the wall.. "I thought I got all of the smart genes, but I guess I was wrong."

Rosie playfully stuck her tongue out at me. "Very funny, Harp. Now be careful with that paint line. You don't want to get green on the ceiling or else we'll have to redo it."

Yeah, yeah, I thought, as I attempted to steady my hand so that the paint line between the wall and ceiling would be perfectly straight.

"So, Harper, I've been reading your blog lately," my mom said. Her voice was suspiciously neutral.

"Oh yeah?" I inquired, turning around on the ladder, and watching as she pushed her paint roller into the pan on the floor.

Here we go, I thought. *This should be interesting. I'm about to get told how terrible my blog is and how I should have higher standards.*

"I can't tell you how happy it makes me that you aren't posting about your bad dates any more. It's such a nice change to see," Mom said. "It took longer than it should have, but I'm glad you finally came around and saw that your bad dates weren't leading you anywhere."

If that's as close to a compliment that I'm going to get from my mom, then I guess I'm just going to have to be happy with it, I thought as I dipped my brush for more paint.

"Um, thanks, Mom," I said, not really sure what else to say. "It's been a refreshing change, that's for sure."

Rosie had a proud and smug look on her face. Clearly, she wanted to be praised for "introducing" me to Gabe. But I wasn't going to give her that, at least not yet. It was a total fluke that Rosie had happened to write to the one guy online who wasn't crazy. I doubted she could repeat that kind of success even if she wanted to.

"I think Harper might have found *the one*," Rosie said to Mom, speaking as though I wasn't standing right there in the room with them. I rolled my eyes at the both of them.

"I sure do hope so," Mom replied. "How exciting would that be?"

"Pretty darn exciting," I mumbled. "I'm so glad to have my life validated by the two of you."

Then Mom turned to me, her smile widening with whatever crazy thoughts were bouncing around in her mind.

"Just wait, Harper," she promised. "Pretty soon, Rosie and I will be helping to paint *your* baby's nursery! How exciting is that?"

I nearly dropped my paintbrush. "Mom, please don't do this. There's no need to plan for my future kids quite yet."

"Oh, honey," Mom laughed. "I've been planning for your future kids since you were born."

If I rolled my eyes any more, they were going to roll right out of my head. Although, kids with Gabe didn't sound half bad. He'd probably make an amazing dad.

"Harp, you missed a spot," Rosie said, pointing toward the wall behind me.

I turned around and quickly fixed the tiny spot that I had missed with the green paint, glad for some sort of distraction.

"I'm glad you guys are excited for me," I said. "It's just that I don't want you to be *overly* excited, you know? Gabe is a great guy, but that doesn't automatically mean that he's the one for me."

"That may be true, honey," Mom said. "But regardless, I'm just happy that you didn't end up using that Kindling Dating just to get more awful dates for your blog. I'm proud of you for using it in the way it was meant to be used."

Rosie nodded with an in-agreement look on her face. I

couldn't help but to roll my eyes yet again. There was no way around it. Rosie and my mom were joined at the hip. No matter what, I'd always end up looking like the black sheep of the family.

I wasn't looking for an argument, though. I had merely come over to my sister's house to see if there was a way to help her out, since her baby would be coming very soon. So I just smiled and turned around to continue my painting.

As I perfected my brush strokes, I thought back to the day when Rosie had announced she'd signed me up for the site. I was kind of angry and annoyed by it initially, but now, as I thought about Gabe, I realized that her signing me up was one of the best things that had ever happened to me. I supposed I could actually thank her for it. But not yet.

Not until I knew for sure that my relationship with Gabe was solid. Then, and only then, would I thank Rosie for pretending to be me on a dating site. But I knew nothing ever turned out as simple as that for me.

CHAPTER 17

*D*inner had been amazing. Spectacular. Delicious. I'd never tasted sushi as fresh or well prepared as I had tonight. Gabe certainly knew how to pick a restaurant, that was for sure.

As soon as we stepped into his house, Gabe kissed me. Our hands had been all over each other at dinner, but we had done our best to keep it appropriate. Now we were back at home, though, and we had total freedom again.

With our lips locked, I reached up and began to undo the buttons of his dress shirt. With just the top part open, I placed my hands onto his bare chest, getting turned on instantly. His muscular pectorals did it to me every time.

Gabe stepped forward and gently pressed me against the wall near the living room. He then broke our kiss and looked down my body.

"You have no idea how hard it was to be a gentleman at dinner with you wearing that."

I smiled flirtatiously and gently pushed my chest out to accentuate my cleavage. The tiny black dress made me feel so sexy and clearly Gabe noticed. He hadn't taken his eyes off of me all dinner. It felt so good to be the center of his attention.

His eyes dilated as he leaned in to kiss the top of my breasts. I tilted my head back, looking up toward the ceiling as I pressed my body toward him. He wasn't the only one who had been thinking about things other than food while at dinner. I had been waiting anxiously the entire evening to get him back home. I wanted him just as badly as he wanted me.

"Take me to the bedroom," I whispered.

Gabe looked up at me, with lust-filled eyes. Then he lifted me up, carrying me across the house and toward the master bedroom at the opposite end. He set me down on the floor in front of the bed and then undid the rest of the buttons on his shirt, letting it fall off of his shoulders.

Something about the way he looked when he was just wearing dress slacks turned me on beyond belief. It made me feel so naughty, like I had convinced him to get undressed after a business meeting or something.

"Why do you have to be so sexy?" I whispered.

Gabe half-smiled, then stepped close to me. His hands landed on my hips and he gripped the material of my dress, causing it to slide upward on my thighs. I loved it when he wanted me like this, and each time we had had sex since we started dating, I began to see this side of him more and more.

"We both know that I'm not the sexy one here," he responded, bringing his lips to the outside of my neck.

My jaw dropped as Gabe nibbled at the sensitive skin just below my ear. It sent goose bumps popping up over my body. He knew that I loved it when he did it. It was one thing that would send me over the top every time.

While he kissed and nipped at my neck, I pulled my

dress down and stepped out of it, rendering me nearly naked with the exception of my panties and bra. When Gabe pulled away, the expression on his face was priceless. He was practically drooling over me. He didn't say anything, he just brought his lips to mine and we enjoyed an electrifying kiss. My hands drifted all over his upper body. His skin, his muscles, his scent; all of it turned me on. It made me ache for him and caused me to become wet with craving.

I reached forward and undid Gabe's belt, letting his pants drop to his ankles. Then I placed my fingers over the bulge that had grown under his boxer briefs. He was so hard already. He let out a guttural moan and gently broke our kiss as I dragged my fingertips over the front of his underwear, focusing on his sensitive tip.

He exhaled, looking into my eyes as I touched him. Then he reached forward and unclasped my bra, exposing my front. He fondled my chest and at the same time, leaned in to kiss my nipples. My body exploded with pleasure, as he used his magnificent tongue in just the right way, causing the sensitive nubs atop my breasts to grow firm.

"Gabe," I whispered.

I wanted to feel him. So I pulled down his underwear with one hand and then gripped his shaft. He let out another moan as I stroked his length, all the way from his base to his tip.

"Oh, my God," he growled.

Gabe slipped my panties off and then placed his hands over my bare behind. He took a step forward and I felt him slide between my thighs. The friction from the top of his cock created a burst of pleasure and a gasp escaped my throat. With just another step forward, Gabe laid me down on top of the bed. He was fully erect, just outside of my sex.

It was beyond tempting to just let him go ahead, but I knew we needed to play it safe.

"Condom?" I asked.

"Yes," he said.

He quickly grabbed a condom from his dresser and slipped it on. He resumed his position immediately.

I reached forward and gripped his shaft, pulling him inside of me. As he entered, a deep wave of ecstasy filled me from head to toe, causing my eyes to roll into the back of my head and my back to arch.

"Yes," I groaned. "Yes..."

For some reason, the pleasure was even more intense than any other time we'd had sex up to that point. Maybe it was because of the sexual tension that had built up during dinner? Or maybe I was just falling for the guy and the emotional bond we had created made the sex that much more amazing? I didn't know. All that I was certain of was that something about *this* time was even more passionate and incredible than the others.

Gabe bucked his hips forward, entering me fully with each press of his body. My back was arched as he increased pace, pounding me hard and filling me with a rush of bliss.

This is exactly what I wanted all evening. I could have probably skipped dinner and gone straight to this.

My legs wrapped around his waist, pulling him into me even deeper and causing the intensity to increase. I let out a squeal with each of his powerful thrusts, unable to contain myself. It felt too amazing. It was more than just physical pleasure, though. There was a connection between us that seemed to become expressed more fully when we made love. Sex with Gabe was distinctly different than any other sex I had ever had.

When I opened my eyes, I took a moment to just admire

him. The way his muscles flexed with his movements and the intense look of lust in his green eyes. I still found it hard to believe that I had landed such a sexy man. I must have done something right at some point in my life.

The position felt amazing, but I wanted more. I wanted him in every way, not just like this. It was one of those nights when I was just feeling naughty and wasn't afraid to show it.

"Baby, let me turn around," I said.

Gabe slowed his pace and then nodded. As soon as he pulled out, I flipped around and bent over in front of him. He stepped forward, gripping my hips with both hands as he entered me once more to resume the pleasure.

"Oh, God, yes," I muttered.

This position felt even more incredible. I loved how his strong hands gripped my hips, pulling me onto his length. It made me feel like he was in control and there was something about that I really enjoyed during sex. There were times when I liked being the one in charge, but this wasn't one of them. I wanted him to take the lead.

My breasts swayed underneath me to the cadence of our lovemaking. I pressed against him, enjoying the way his body slammed against mine, each plunge delivering another deep wave of ecstasy. My body was on fire. Every cell exploded with sensation. My hands trembled as they gripped the pillow in front of me. I was overflowing with euphoria and I had to remind myself to breathe.

It came on quickly, almost unexpectedly fast. But the next thing I knew, I was climaxing. I closed my eyes and buried my face into the pillow, letting out a low moan as I rode the roller coaster up, feeling the intensity of the pleasure peak. I trembled over Gabe's cock as a deep satisfaction filled me from head to toe. I noticed every inch of him now, as the orgasm had made me temporarily more sensitive down there.

When my breathing returned to normal, I looked over my shoulder. Gabe had desire written on over his face, as his hands moved upward along my back. He then slowed his pace down and finally pulled out.

"The shower," he said. "I want you in the shower."

I flipped over, letting out a soft giggle.

"You're so bad," I flirted.

Gabe growled playfully and then lifted me up, carrying me straight to the oversized shower. He turned on the water and we stepped inside. Gabe didn't hesitate. He turned me around so that my back was facing him and then gently pressed onto my shoulders. I bent over slightly, holding myself up against the tile wall as the hot water poured around us.

Within a moment, he was back inside. I let out a groan as the pleasure rose in me once again. This was the first time we'd done anything like this in the shower, but I liked it. It was unconventional and sexy. It was new and adventurous.

Gabe's hands slid over my skin, which was now slick with water. He touched my breasts, gliding his fingers over them as they swayed below me. It wasn't more than a few minutes before I heard Gabe let out groan. I looked over my shoulder, watching his face contort and flush as he closed his eyes and leaned his head back. He was about to climax.

An animal-sounding grunt escaped his lips and immediately after, he pressed into me and held himself there. His length trembled inside as he released all of the sexual energy that he had repressed the entire evening. The erotic tension was liberated in one glorious climax. It took a moment, but Gabe finally opened his eyes and drew in a breath. His orgasm made him look dazed, yet extremely content.

I spun around and placed my hands onto his shoulders, giving him a sensual kiss. When I pulled away, I looked him in the eyes. "We should do the shower thing more often. I like this."

Gabe's hands moved up and down my sides as the water poured around us.

"Yes, we definitely should," he agreed, with a playful smirk.

We finished our shower and then got out. I wrapped myself up in one of Gabe's comfy white towels, and then went to the bedroom. We curled up on the bed together and turned on the TV. On the first station was some reality show that neither of us cared about, but we didn't bother to change it. It wasn't what was on the TV that mattered anyway. I only cared that I was laying there with Gabe to watch it. That was enough.

CHAPTER 18

At what point can I stop counting these rendezvous with Gabe as just casual dates? I wondered. *Seems like we've had at least five so far. Are we actually dating yet?*

Gabe was still asleep in his bed, but I had been awake for a while, just relaxing and enjoying the quiet morning in his beautiful house. I had made myself some coffee and a bagel, which I ate out in the living room while casually surfing the Internet and checking on my blog. I was surprised to see how much traffic my website had been getting ever since I started posting about my relationship with Gabe. It seemed that there were plenty of people out there who liked reading about good dates and not just nightmarish ones.

After finishing my coffee, I set my laptop down onto the end table and walked over to open the patio door at the back of his house. From where I stood, I could see the ocean stretched out in front of me. Seagulls flew near the beach, their sounds filling me with nostalgia from a life of growing up near the water. The smell of the salt and sand had already penetrated the air, even though it wasn't even warm outside yet. The scene was beautiful and I began to fully understand why Gabe had chosen to buy this house out of the others. Nobody else on the island had a view quite like this.

I'm one lucky girl to be here right now, I thought, as I leaned against the door jam.

I was wearing one of Gabe's t-shirts as pajamas. It was perfectly worn-in and soft as it caressed my skin. The morning breeze blew gently over me, and I caught of whiff of Gabe's scent coming from the shirt. It caused me to smile warmly and instantly made me want to be near him. So I slid across the hardwood floors in my socks, making my way back to the bedroom for a morning cuddle.

He even looks sexy when he's asleep, I thought as I entered the room.

Gabe was laying on his back in the bed, with his torso exposed. The sun poured into his window, blanketing him with light. I stood there for just a moment, shaking my head in awe that my life was beginning to become so amazing. I thought for sure things wouldn't ever turn out even close to this, and yet, here I was, looking at the man of my dreams as he slept.

He was amazing to look at, no doubt. But I didn't want to stand there for more than a few seconds. After that, staring at someone while they sleep begins to register on the creep-o-meter and I refused to be that woman.

I approached the bed and crawled under the covers, snuggling up next to Gabe. He stirred in his sleep and then partially opened his eyes.

"Good morning," I said.

"Morning, beautiful," he whispered back.

Then he wrapped his arm over my shoulder and pulled me close. I laid my head on his chest and closed my eyes, immediately soothed by the rhythmic sound of his breathing.

"How long have you been awake?" he asked, his voice hoarse with sleep.

"Not very long," I said. "The sun woke me up a little while ago and so I made some coffee and messed around on the Internet. I was thinking of trying to get some actual work done, but it felt too good to be lazy."

"What time is it?" Gabe asked, not bothering to move to even look at his watch.

"A little after nine."

"You were up before nine on a Sunday?" he replied. "You're insane."

"Yeah, I know," I replied with a chuckle. "I'm an early bird, you know that."

Gabe kissed the top of my head and began to gently drag his fingers over my back.

Is this what it feels like to be happy? I wondered. *Like truly, stupidly happy? The kind of happy they talk about in books, where the girl dances around with a smile on her face, excited for every day of her life?*

That's what I was beginning to feel like. I was on cloud nine every day, ever since my first date with Gabe. And each day that I spent with him, things only got better.

I drew imaginary lines over his pectorals as we laid in the morning sun, wondering what it would be like to wake up with him *every* day, not just the days after a date.

I think I could seriously get used to this, I thought with a smile.

Then a sinking feeling filled my gut. It felt like a punch in the stomach.

My blog could put all of this at risk, I realized. *All those bad dates that I never mentioned. The lie of omission about what I do for work... not to mention if Gabe found out that I've been posting everything about our dates online and letting strangers read about it, he'd probably be pissed. I wouldn't blame him either. I'd be angry if he was doing something like that.*

It was the first time I really felt like I had something to lose because of the website. I mean the blog was running well, and that made me happy. But at what expense? It wasn't easy for me to justify traffic to the website if it took potentially losing the best thing I've ever had in my life to get it.

"Did you fall back asleep?" Gabe whispered, distracting me from my thoughts for a moment.

"No, I'm just thinking," I said, trying to ignore the ball of ice forming in my stomach.

"Did you eat yet?" he asked, still not moving. "We should have breakfast."

"I had a bagel with my coffee, but that was a while ago," I murmured, my thoughts still on my blog.

"How does breakfast in bed sound?" he asked.

I lifted my head from his chest and looked up at him.

"You want to have it delivered or something?" I replied.

"No way," he said, as he slowly sat up.

I sat up with him and watched as he crawled out of bed, still in his glorious nakedness from the night before. He slipped on his white robe and turned to face the bed.

"I'll make you breakfast," he said, with a proud smile. "You just lay there and relax. I'll have it ready in a few minutes."

The expression that fell across my face must have made me look like a total goof. It was a combination of joy, love, and pure shock. Nobody had ever made me breakfast in bed. In fact, I don't think even my mother had, even when I was a kid. And now Gabe, the wealthy guy who lived on an island, was going to cook for me? If there was a cloud ten, then I just landed on it.

"You're the best," I announced. "I'd love that."

"Good," he replied. "How does scrambled eggs, toast and hash browns sound?"

"Absolutely amazing." I narrowed my eyes. "Is Bastian coming over? Did you plan this?"

Gabe laughed. "No, I'd thought I'd try it myself," he said as he left the room. "As you know, I may not be the best cook of all time, but I firmly believe that I have it in me not to screw up scrambled eggs. It's impossible to screw up scrambled eggs, right?"

"I don't think it would matter even if the scrambled eggs were burnt to a crisp," I said. "The fact that you're making them at all is what matters. Thanks, Gabe."

He disappeared around the corner and a moment later, I listened to the sound of him making breakfast. The clanging of pots and pans, and the occasional curse word, as he did his best, which was good enough for me.

Do I love this guy? I asked myself, falling back into the pillow. *Can I see myself finally committing to a man? Is he really the one for me?*

My mom would have loved to ask me these same questions and I would have probably cringed if she had. But there I was, asking them to myself and desperately wanting to know the answers. I didn't have the answers, though. I was stuck with only feelings. My heart was quickly taking over and it was a sensation that I wasn't used to.

Is it possible to truly love someone after just two months of dating?

The logical side of my mind kicked in, trying to squeeze in a question, but the sound of my heart drowned it out.

Of course it's possible, I thought. *Why not? Some people get married after just a couple of weeks of knowing each other. Why couldn't it happen?*

A few minutes later, the sound of a crashing pan coming from the kitchen caused me to jump and sit up in the bed, breaking my daydreaming.

"Are you okay out there?" I called out.

"Yeah, I'm fine," Gabe responded. "It just might be a few more minutes on the hash browns. There was a little accident."

I giggled softly as I pulled the blankets up to my chin, snuggling in the warmth that Gabe had left on the bed.

"Don't worry about the hash browns!" I said. "Eggs and toast is fine with me."

A moment later, Gabe popped around the corner with two plates.

"I'm glad you said that," he told me, looking a little sheepish. "Because I used all of the potatoes I had with the first batch of hash browns, and they just ended up on the floor."

He looked so darn cute, standing there in his robe with that boyish smile. He was a man in every sense of the word, but sometimes the boy in him shined through. I loved it. I loved absolutely everything about it. There was a sense of innocence in him that only attracted me more.

"I hope you like your toast with butter and strawberry jam," he said, as he walked over to hand me my plate.

"That's perfect," I replied. "It smells great, Gabe. Thank you."

"You're welcome," he said, walking over to the other side of the bed and crawling next to me.

We sat there, leaning against the headboard and eating breakfast. It wasn't a five star hotel and we weren't eating eggs benedict or anything fancy. But it didn't matter. I wouldn't have wanted any of those things anyway. I wanted exactly what I had right there; Gabe, some scrambled eggs and burnt toast, and the sound of the ocean coming in through the window.

This is what I call a perfect morning, I thought.

CHAPTER 19

Gabe and I had just finished our last bite of breakfast when his cell phone on the nightstand began to ring. He looked over at it and then toward me. "I *really* don't want to answer that."

"Well, do you have to?" I asked.

With a sigh, he reached over and pulled the phone off of the charger before looking at the screen.

"I probably should," he said. "It's one of the guys I work with and he doesn't usually call unless there's a legitimate reason, especially on a Sunday."

"Go ahead and answer it," I replied. "I'll just go hang out in the living room. Maybe I can get a little work done while you're on your call."

Gabe leaned in and gave me a quick peck on the lips before getting out of bed. "Okay, I'll try to make it fast. I don't want to waste this perfect Sunday morning taking care of business stuff."

"Take your time, Gabe. It's no big deal. The Internet is a very big place and there's plenty there to keep me occupied."

"You're the best," he said, as he lifted the phone to his ear and stepped out of the bedroom.

"Hey buddy, what's up?" Gabe said, as he walked away.

His voice faded out as he made his way upstairs to have his phone conversation. I got up and went straight to the living room to grab my laptop.

Might as well get some work done, I thought. *Maybe I'll go sit outside so that I can enjoy this belly full of breakfast and the morning sunshine at the same time.*

I stepped out onto the patio and got comfortable on one of the padded lawn chairs. I was all ready to get some work done. But when I opened my laptop, I noticed that my battery was down to just twelve percent.

Crap. There's no way that's enough battery power to allow me to aimlessly peruse the internet for funny cat videos while trying to avoid any actual work, I thought.

Of course, since I was at Gabe's house and not my own, I didn't have my laptop charger with me. It seemed that there would be no work getting accomplished or cat videos getting watched that morning.

Unless...

I set the laptop down on a nearby lounger and then stood up.

Maybe Gabe has a charger in his office. I'm pretty sure he has the kind of laptop that I do, I thought.

He was still upstairs on his phone call and I could barely hear him talking as I poked my head back into the living room. I wanted to ask him if I could borrow his charger, but I really didn't want to interrupt him during a business call.

I guess I can at least go try to find it myself, I thought. *If he has a charger that will work, it will surely be in his office. At least that's the most likely place I can think of.*

Gabe's home office was located on the main level near

the front door. I walked toward it and when I got there, I hesitated. It felt weird going in there without his permission. I mean sure, we were sleeping together and all that, but I didn't feel like that alone gave me enough leverage to enter his office without him knowing.

I'll just poke my head in really quick and see if there's a charger, I thought to myself, justifying my intrusion.

I turned the handle and walked inside. His office was just as beautiful as the rest of the home, with dark mahogany furniture and beautiful artwork. In the center of the room was a giant desk and on it, was his laptop, which sat opened with the screen saver running.

"Perfect," I said, as I approached the desk to borrow the charger from his computer.

When I got close, though, I looked down and noticed a piece of paper sitting next to the computer. It caught my eye, and not because I'm a curious person or the type who enjoys snooping. The paper drew my attention, because on it, I saw a smiling picture of Gabe. I recognized it immediately, because it was the same photo he had used in his profile on the dating site where I had first seen him.

If I had had the willpower, I would have turned around and marched straight out of that office without looking at that paper for another second. But I couldn't. Once I saw something interesting, I couldn't stop myself.

I slipped around to the other side of his desk and took a seat in the black leather chair. Then I leaned in, taking a closer look. On the paper, there was the picture of Gabe, with a note scribbled underneath it. It said *"Hey, Gabe, do you want to use this same picture for the ad? This is the one you're using as a profile picture currently. Wasn't sure if that was a good idea or a bad idea to use the same one. Lemme know. –Bastian"*

"What the hell?" I whispered.

My eyes moved downward on the page, where there were some more notes written in the same handwriting, so I knew that it was Bastian. They read, "*So we're thinking of running this advertisement on multiple platforms, right? We still need to figure out which photo we're going to use so that I can get it formatted. Should we have the one with just you or the one with you and Harper? There are some examples on the back of this page. Please let me know which one you like the best and I'll get this rolling ASAP.*"

When I saw my own name written there, my stomach turned. I wasn't even entirely sure what I was upset about yet, but I had a feeling I was being betrayed somehow.

What is all this? What is Bastian asking?

I slowly flipped over the paper. On the back of the page, was a picture of Gabe and I standing on his patio with the ocean view as our backdrop. Gabe had taken the selfie of the two of us just a week prior. I remembered it precisely, because I loved the photo so much that I decided to use it as my profile picture on Facebook.

Only this particular version of the picture had been altered slightly from the one that was familiar to me. Written in white letters across the bottom, it read, "If the mathematician behind The Kindling Dating website and the blogger behind Never After can find love here..."

My knees turned to gelatin and I collapsed into the office chair. I felt my heart thud quickly behind my rib cage, causing my blood pressure to rise and a knot of anxiety to build in my stomach.

A little further down the page was a different picture of Gabe and I. This one, Bastian had taken of us while he was making us dinner the first time I visited Gabe's home. I hadn't even realized he'd snapped a picture of us that night, but I could tell by my outfit in the photo that this was when it was from. It had Gabe and I sitting on the couch in the living room, laughing while we sipped our wine.

This one had writing on it that read, "The creator of Kindling Dating met the love of his life on his own website. It can do the same for you..."

His own website?

I glanced around the office, feeling a wave of dizziness fill me as the realization of the truth began to sink in. On the wall near the front door, I noticed a plaque with Gabe's name inscribed on it. Above his name, it read, "Most Successful Internet Entrepreneur of the Year."

I thought he was a computer programmer. What the hell is going on?

My mind flowed with rapid thoughts and my heart rate continued to increase as rage flowed into my veins.

A picture on the wall was of Gabe and two other men at a ribbon cutting ceremony. One of them was Bastian, but I didn't recognize the other. Behind them was the Kindling Dating building downtown. Beside it was a newspaper article emblazoned: *Three Entrepreneurs Open Kindling Dating and Become Overnight Billionaires!*

It was then that I noticed all the Kindling Dating logos on everything.

"Gabe is the creator of Kindling Dating?" I whispered to myself. "This has to be a freaking joke."

Not only was it starting to become clear that he owned and ran the dating website, but he was also using *our* relationship to create an ad for that website. He was using *us* to garner more business for *himself*.

Any happy thoughts or feelings I had enjoyed that morning were gone just as fast as the fog lifted from the shore of the island. If what I was looking at was to be believed, then Gabe was the founder and creator of the dating site that he had used to meet me. He had created the algorithm in the site, along with all of the questions used to match people up with each other.

I looked back at the photos of us, which now looked more like cheap advertisements than they did loving photos of a potential couple. I didn't want to believe that what I was seeing was true. But it's very difficult not to believe something that's printed in full color on high gloss when you're still in the soft-focus, smudgy lines of a lazy Sunday morning. The images contrasted so blatantly in my mind that even though I tried to convince myself I was having a bad dream, I knew in my heart that I wasn't. This was real. This was actually happening.

I read and re-read the advertisements, feeling my stomach turn a little more as the gravity of the situation set in. Just an hour earlier I was thinking I might be in love and then there I was, questioning if I even knew Gabe on any level at all.

Is everything he told me a complete lie? Is he even a computer programmer? I just thought he happened to be wealthy, maybe because he was good with money. I didn't know he owned the biggest dating site in the world, the same one he used to meet me.

What had me the most upset about learning all of this, though, was that it completely cheapened my thoughts of being in love. It was like all of our time together was for nothing more than the creation of some advertisement.

Was all of this a set-up?

I couldn't help but to wonder if this had been Gabe's plan all along. Maybe he had found out about my blog and realized that a website like mine could be great publicity for his own site. Then, when he saw me on Kindling Dating, he knew he had to take the opportunity to meet me in order to make that happen. It was just too perfect.

Of course, this was all complete speculation and I didn't know for sure what was going on. But it didn't matter. Whether these advertisements were just a drawn out, conniving plan, or not, it didn't change anything. The seed of doubt was planted. Now I had seen a glimpse of the truth and there was no turning back. The sunlight had cut through the fog and it couldn't be undone.

I pushed the paper aside and stood up from Gabe's office chair. Then I marched toward the door with anger in my steps. Many of the details about what was going on were still unclear, but I knew all that I really needed to know.

It's over. I'm done with him. As soon as I can get past this crushing feeling in my chest and gather everything for my overnight bag, I'm walking out of his house and never turning back. He just lost the best thing he could have had.

With tears welling in my eyes, I left the office and made my way toward the bedroom to gather my things. Gabe was still upstairs, talking on his phone. The sound of his voice was now much less soothing and only brought with it the emotional pain of being lied to for two whole months.

CHAPTER 20

*A*fter storming out of Gabe's office, I went back to the bedroom and got dressed as quickly as possible. I was teeming with emotion, but I didn't want to let out a single sob. I could save that for later, when I could enjoy a pint if ice cream and a few days of binge watching my favorite TV show. But for now, I needed to keep it together and act tough.

So once I was dressed, I gathered my makeup from his countertop in his bathroom and tossed everything into my overnight bag. To think, I was considering what it would be like to spend my life with the guy and now I was doing everything possible to speed up the process of leaving his house for good.

I can't believe this. I should have known that it would only be a matter of time before something like this would happen to me, I thought. Why did I fool myself into thinking I could actually meet a decent guy?

I zipped up my bag and tossed it over my shoulder. Before leaving the bedroom, I took one last look at the bed, where the blankets were still messed up from us cuddling that morning. My heart hurt at the thought I'd never sleep next to him again and that everything I had considered to be "love" was nothing more than a bunch of hogwash.

There is no love, I told myself. *Love is just a word used to sell advertising on dating websites. "Find Love" or "Let Love Find You" or however you want to say it to make it sound better, it still doesn't mean a thing.*

With all of my belongings in hand, I spun around and left the room, marching toward the front door. I didn't hear Gabe talking upstairs on the phone any longer, which was fine. I had no intention of saying goodbye or explaining my reason for my leaving. My plan was to walk about that door and block his phone number and email. Basically, I was just going to cut him out of my life completely. I figured it would hurt a little less if I took control of the situation.

But when I got to the front door and opened it up, I heard Gabe call from the top of the stairs.

"Babe, where are you going? I'm off the call now," he shouted down.

I couldn't bear to turn around to look at him, so I just stepped outside and walked toward the sidewalk so I could call a cab. Gabe yelled out behind me and I heard him run down the stairs inside.

"Harper, hold up," he said, as he followed me out the door. "Where are you headed? The day is just getting started, there's no need to leave yet. I'm sorry about having to take that call."

I continued to walk, setting my jaw and keeping my pace.

"Harper!" he shouted, as he ran up beside me. "Are you okay?"

"No," I stated flatly.

"What's going on?" Gabe asked, as he positioned himself in front of me, blocking my path.

"Let me go, Gabe," I said.

"If you want to go, you can," he said. "I'm just really confused right now. What's going on? Are you mad that I took that phone call?"

This was my chance to confront him about what I had seen in his office, so I decided to take it. It seemed he wasn't going to let me leave without an explanation anyway.

"The *phone call*? I don't give a crap about this morning's phone call, Gabe," I snapped. "This has nothing to do with that."

"Well then what is it?" He seemed legitimately concerned, but clearly confused about what had me upset.

"I can't believe you were going to use our relationship as an advertisement for your stupid website," I growled, my voice growing in volume with each word.

Gabe's face turned ghostly pale and I watched as he drew in a nervous breath.

"Harper," he began.

"Shut up, Gabe. I don't want to hear it," I told him. "Move, please."

"Let me explain," he said, holding out his hands.

"Explain what? You want to explain to me that you're the creator of the website we met each other on? You want to hash out the details of your life a little bit, so that I actually know who you are. I feel like I've been dating a stranger," I yelled at him. "I thought you were a computer guy or something. I didn't know that you were the owner of the biggest online dating site in the world. You'd think that something like that would have been worth mentioning. Unless, of course, you were trying to hide it for some reason."

Gabe opened his mouth and then closed it, took a deep breath and placed his hands onto his hips.

"I was going to tell you," he replied.

"When? When were you going to tell me, Gabe?" I asked. "After you posted the advertisement online, the one that used the same photo of us that I cherished so much? Is that when? Or were you going to wait until I found out on my own? Why don't you just tell me the truth and admit that you had no intention of *ever* telling me? You hoped I'd never find out and we both know it."

My heart was racing now and I practically saw red. If it hadn't been for the overnight bag in one hand and my cell phone in the other, I probably would have slapped the guy. He'd managed to break my heart in one fell swoop, all by deliberately hiding information from me.

"I'm sorry I didn't tell you," he said, pacing his words to keep himself calm. "I was going to tell you and I planned on doing so sooner rather than later-"

"Stop. Just stop," I interrupted him. "I only really want to know one thing. Why did you bother with it? Why make a profile on your own website? Was this whole thing between us just a set up so that you'd have good content for an ad?"

Gabe looked up, collecting his thoughts or maybe creating the lie he was about to spill out. I couldn't be sure. I felt like I didn't know him at all any more.

"I created a profile on the website to see what it was like to be on there. I've spent years developing it, but hadn't ever put it to use," he admitted.

"So I was market research?" I asked, wanting to scream and hit things.

"No, Harper. That's not it at all!" He ran his hands through his dark hair in frustration. "I didn't plan for this."

"You know what Gabe, go to hell. Go straight to hell." I

was vibrating I was so angry. I felt like I was about to explode like a nuclear bomb. "You and Bastian and your website and this mansion can all disappear for all I care. I'm gone."

I pushed past him and continued my trek toward the sidewalk, opening up my phone to call a cab.

"If we're going to be spilling out all our secrets, why don't we talk about *your* little website too, Harper?" Gabe called after me. "Seems like that would only be fair."

I stopped in my tracks and turned around to face Gabe once again. He stood at the top of his driveway with his arms crossed. His green eyes burned me like fire.

"I wasn't the only one with a secret," he said.

Jerk. Total jerk.

My emotion was now running my decisions. I marched back up the driveway and pushed his chest, causing him to take a step back.

"Yeah, I blogged about our dates," I admitted. "But I *never* would have done something to sell you out. What you did to me was a hundred times worse."

"You blogged with intent, Harper. Your intent was to get traffic to your website," he shrugged, mocking me. "I don't feel like it's that much different than what I did."

"No, my *intent* was to tell the *truth*. And the truth was that I was having the best time of my life with you and I was shocked that I had finally met someone worth investing my time in. *That's* all I ever said to anybody," I yelled at him. My voice cracked. "Clearly, though, everything I said was nothing more than a childish dream. To think, I thought this might actually go somewhere. Too bad it's over now."

"What's that supposed to mean?" he asked, taking a step back. "Just like that? The time we've spent together means nothing?"

"It means absolutely nothing to me now," I said, trying to convince myself more than him. "I'm done, Gabe. You broke my trust and because of that, you lost your chance. Your stupid little algorithms can't help you with this one, can they, Mister *Computer Programmer.*"

The last words came out with a snarky growl, just to emphasize once again how I felt about him in that moment.

Gabe's mouth fell open and then his eyes narrowed to glowing green slits. "You know what? Just leave, Harper. If you're going to act like this, then get out of here."

"My pleasure," I said. "Maybe I'll stop somewhere and order some real food that's not burnt to a crisp. You know, you're in your thirties, Gabe. If you weren't such a spoiled little rich kid, maybe you'd have learned to cook freaking eggs by now. Seriously, get out more. Learn to do things like a regular human being. I'm not sure if you've realized this, but there are people in the world that can't hire out every single aspect of their life. I'm surprised you can even go to the bathroom by yourself. Or do you have a secret bathroom attendant that you haven't told me about? It wouldn't surprise me if you did. It would just be one more thing you tried to hide from me."

He didn't say a word in response but the expression on his face showed that my words were making him angry. Silently, he lifted his hand and pointed toward the street, showing me away from the house. I turned around and walked off, moving quickly to get as far away from him as possible. My hand was shaking as I lifted my phone and called a cab to come pick me up.

What a freaking jerk. I can't believe this, I thought as I stomped down the street. I managed to make it to the end of the block where he couldn't see me anymore before I started to cry.

The tears I had managed to hold back during our argument finally made their way up to my eyes and overflowed down my cheeks. I wiped the first batch away with the back of my hand, but it didn't do any good. More came to replace them and it was only a few seconds later that I couldn't even slow them down. I sobbed hard, unable to keep my emotion at bay any longer.

The crushing pain in my chest only became more amplified with each step I took away from Gabe's home. I felt like I had been deceived worse than any other time in my life. When I got to the end of the street I turned back around to take a final glance at his house. He wasn't standing in the driveway any longer and the front door was closed once again.

"This isn't fair," I whispered.

I stepped around the corner and took a seat on the edge of the sidewalk while I waited for my cab. I wanted things to be different. A part of me really wished I hadn't ever walked into his office to see that piece of paper. Ignorance would have been bliss. If my laptop had been charged and I hadn't gone into his office, then I would have been cuddling with him right then, still happy out of my head with how things were going.

But things never seem to go my way, I thought.

Gabe was the one person who I had finally opened my heart to. Sure, we had only been dating for two months, but it was long enough for me to wonder if I actually loved the guy and that was something that hadn't happened in a long time. I thought he was different. I thought that somehow he'd be the one to change my mind about how awful relationships were and how much they can hurt. Apparently, I was wrong.

Luckily, it wasn't too long before the cab pulled up. I

stood up from my seat on the curb, dusted myself off and crawled into the backseat of the car.

"Good morning, ma'am," the cabby said. "Where can I take you?"

I sniffled and attempted to wipe my tears away once again before responding. "Anywhere but here."

"Is everything okay, ma'am?" he asked, as he turned around in his seat to get a look at me.

"I'm fine," I replied. "Can we just drive?"

The last thing I needed was for Gabe to look out his window and see me just sitting in a cab. I didn't want him thinking I was even debating whether or not I should leave.

"Sure thing, ma'am. I can drive," he said. "But where are we going?"

I thought about it for a moment. I wasn't really sure where I wanted to go. If I went home, I knew I'd be stuck with only my thoughts. That wasn't something that would be good for me. I'd end up super depressed, wrapping myself in blankets, while crying my eyes out in despair. Plus, I'd likely end up calling Gabe at some point, just to try to ease the pain in my gut from the breakup. So home wasn't a good option.

My mother's? I thought. *Wait, no, that's a horrible idea.*

It was already hard enough that I had just broken up with a man I thought I loved, but I knew I would also get an earful about it once the news reached my mom. I could already hear the "I told you so" coming from her mouth. I considered going to Rosie's place, but I knew she was busy getting ready for the baby. Plus, she would likely hit me with the same grief as my mother. Both Rosie and my mom would have found some way to turn the situation against me, making it seem like my fault that things didn't work out with Gabe.

"Ma'am?" the cabby asked again, starting to look more impatient instead of compassionate.

"Take me to the airport," I suddenly said, as the idea flashed into my mind.

The cabby nodded and pulled away from the curb. My overnight bag was already packed and I even had an extra outfit, along with all of my makeup. I had no reason to go home, so I made the decision right then to fly to Orlando.

If there's one person who can help me through this, it's Cora. She's the only one who can make me feel right now. The only one.

CHAPTER 21

The plane ride to Orlando only took less than an hour, but it felt like an eternity. I spent the entire trip trying to hide my sobs, but of course it was impossible. Luckily, I had sat in the window seat and was able to face away from everyone while I cried, but I still knew that people were looking at me. The older lady sitting next to me even asked if there was anything she could do to help. I responded with, "If you can make men honest, that would help." She just laughed and said, "I don't think there's anything I can do about that one."

My makeup was ruined, my hair was a mess and the clothes I had on were a day old. Needless to say, I wasn't looking like I was ready to hit the town when I crawled off of the plane. It didn't matter, though. Cora didn't care what I looked like. She wouldn't judge me. That was why I had come to see her in the first place.

I had only taken a few steps out of the front doors of the airport before I heard Cora calling out my name. I hadn't even gotten to the parking lot yet.

"Harper!" she shouted, as she squealed her little Toyota

next to the curb in front of me.

The ball of anxiety in my gut was relieved, even if only a little bit, just by the sight of her. She was the refuge that I needed in my moment of pain.

"Hi, Cora," I said, walking over to her car. "Thank you for agreeing to get together."

"Hey, Harp. You don't have to thank me. I'm happy to do it," she said, hopping out and giving me a quick hug. "I've been wanting to see you anyway and now I finally get to. See, things always end up working out."

I tossed my bags into her trunk before walking around and getting in the passenger seat as Cora started up the engine. Cora smiled at me, pushing her curly black hair out of her eyes before leaning in for another hug.

"It's good to see you, Harper," she said. "I've missed you."

"I've missed you, too," I assured her.

Before pulling away from the curb, she looked me in the eyes. "But I have to say. You look like you've been hit by a bus."

Somehow her comment forced a smile out of me. I playfully pushed her shoulder. "Thanks, Cora. I knew I could count on you for support."

"I'm just giving you a hard time," she said, as she stepped on the gas. "But seriously, a bus. It looks like a bus hit you. Like head on, while you were walking through a parking lot."

"Cora!" I said, as I laughed at her comment. "You're so mean!"

"You know I love you, Harp." She looked over at me, before patting the top of my knee. "And as soon as we get back to my place, you're going to tell me everything that happened with Gabe. We'll get through this together. It's not going to be easy, but I'm here for you."

"Thanks, Cora," I said, as I closed my eyes and tried to relax during the short drive back to her place.

"I HAVEN'T BEEN HERE in forever," I said as Cora let me into her apartment. The small space was familiar, yet different. I could tell she'd replaced her couch and several other pieces of furniture, but at least the ocean artwork all over her walls was the same.

"Too long," she agreed. "You remember Jack, though, right?"

For a fleeting second, I thought she was referring to some guy she was dating. That was, until, the black and white fur ball popped around the corner, mewing at me as he approached.

"Oh, Jack!" I squealed, as I knelt down to pet the cat. "How could I forget about you, Jack?"

He looked up at me, squinting his green eyes as though he were asking who the hell I was and what I was doing in his castle. But after a few pets, he seemed to be perfectly accepting of my presence. It wasn't long before he was purring like crazy while digging his claws into the carpet. Cora had named him after her favorite billionaire, Jack Saunders, which I had told her was crazy, but she didn't care.

"So, Harp, what can I get you to drink?" Cora asked, walking into her kitchen.

"Maybe just a coffee and an orange juice," I said. I didn't really feel like having anything.

"Coffee and orange juice is not going to make you feel any better," she replied. "What do you want to *drink*? Like what kind of adult beverage would you like to help wash away the pain of your breakup?"

"It's like eleven in the morning, Cora," I said, with a smile. "Isn't it kind of socially unacceptable to drink at this hour?"

"Well, when you go around labeling certain times of the day like that, then yes. I guess we'll wait an hour before drinking, so as to appease the gods of social acceptance." She spun around and stepped back into the kitchen. "In the meantime, though, I'll get you your coffee and orange juice."

"Thanks, lady," I said, as I took a seat on the white leather lounger in the living room.

Jack jumped up onto my lap immediately and I resumed giving him pets. It wasn't long before he curled up and fell asleep on top of me.

"At least *someone* loves me," I joked.

Cora popped around the corner, carrying a mug of coffee and a glass of orange juice.

"*Two* people love you," she corrected me. "Jack and myself. That's enough, isn't it?"

"I wish it was," I joked back, as I took the drinks from her and set them on the end table next to the lounge chair. "Unfortunately, Jack only loves me for the pets I give him."

"Yeah, same here. And for the fact that I feed him." She frowned and shrugged. "Maybe that's all love is, though."

"What? Feeding someone?" I asked. "That's love?"

"Sure, why not?" Cora shrugged as she sat cross-legged on the love seat at the other side of the room. "It's as good of an explanation as anything else I've heard."

I sighed. Just talking about love caused a fresh stab of emotion to enter my heart as the image of Gabe flashed in my mind. Cora noticed my pain instantly.

"Tell me everything," she said.

"It hurts too much to talk about it," I replied as I held back the sobs threatening to burst out of me again. I thought I had gotten them all out on the plane, but apparently not.

"Look, Harper, sometimes you have to work through the pain by working through the pain," Cora said softly. "There's no other way around it."

"I know, you're right. It's just hard," I sniffled. "I just can't believe this actually happened."

"Can you tell me what exactly it was that happened?" she asked. "The only thing I gathered from your call this morning was that Gabe was a total jerk, you're done with men and you're coming to see me in Orlando. That's all I've got to work with so far."

"Gabe *is* a total jerk," I agreed. "Cora, I really thought I knew him. He seemed so different than the others, you know? But then I found something in his office that was rather... embarassing."

She scooted up to the edge of the love seat. "Don't tell me he was seeing someone else. I'll fly out there and kick his butt. Nobody does that to my Harper."

"No, no." I shook my head. "That's not what it was."

Cora's eyes widened as she nodded. "Well...?"

"Kindling Dating," I told her.

"What about it?"

"Gabe owns the site." I waited for her reaction but she just looked confused.

"What do mean, he *owns* the site?" she asked. "Like he's very prominent on there? He meets a lot of girls there?"

"No, Cora. Gabe literally *owns* the website. Kindling Dating is *his* creation. I didn't know that until this morning, though. He had told me he was a computer programmer or something along those lines, but he was never specific," I said. I felt so stupid saying it all out loud. "I should have known something was up, though, the first time that I saw his mansion. No cubicle-bound keyboard jockey would have been able to afford a place like his. The guy's a freaking billionaire."

"You're telling me that Gabe, the guy you've been dating, is the *owner* of Kindling Dating and he didn't tell you?" She whistled softly. "Why would he hide something like that?"

I shrugged. "Maybe because he didn't want me to know that he had probably rigged the algorithms to put himself in front of every hot girl on there," I guessed. "Who knows how many other girls he was stringing along?"

Cora listened quietly, letting me vent. "I'm so sorry, Harper."

"But you know what makes me more angry than the fact that he owns the site? The fact that he didn't tell me." My hands balled up into fists and I pressed them into my thighs to keep from hitting something. "If he had just been open with me, then I wouldn't have been mad. I might have been upset at first, but not enough to leave him and never want to see him again."

As the last sentence spilled from my lips, the tears began to flow once again. My heart still ached and talking about it almost seemed to make it worse. The truth of the situation felt more real by the second.

"How did you find out about this then?" she asked once I had stopped sobbing.. "I mean if Gabe didn't tell you."

"I found a piece of paper in his office. On it was a picture of us that he and I had taken on his front porch. Underneath it was some click bait slogan. It said something like 'If the mathematician who created Kindling Dating can meet the woman who writes for Never After, then what can it do for you?'" I started to tear up, thinking of that treasured photograph being used in such a cheap way. She handed me a tissue and I wiped at my face. "Basically, he was going to use our relationship to promote his site."

"No freaking way," she whispered.

"Yea," I muttered. I grabbed another tissue.

"Why would he do something like that, especially without telling you?" Cora asked, shaking her head. "And how did he even find out about your blog?"

"The guy's got more money than anyone I've ever met. I'm sure it wasn't hard," I said with a shrug. "All he'd have to do is a little searching around on the Internet and he could have found out everything he wanted to about me. Or he might have hired someone to make sure that the guy dating a billionaire isn't a total wackjob. I'm not sure when or how he found out, but he figured it out somehow."

I wish that I had done the same thing with him. A simple Internet search could have given me all of the information that I needed to know about him, I thought.

"I'm so sorry, Harper," Cora said, as she got off of the love seat and came to sit next to me. She wrapped an arm around me and leaned her head against my shoulder. Her touch felt soothing and allowed even more of my emotion to vent. I began to cry. It wasn't just the choking back of sobs like I had done on the airplane, though. I cried hard this time. I turned toward Cora and pressed my face into her shoulder, letting the tears flow. The dam had broken.

"It's okay, lady, I'm here," Cora said, as she stroked my hair. "Jack and I are here for you. Who needs Gabe anyway?"

Logically, I knew she was right. Why would I want to be with someone who hid the truth from me? But my heart didn't care what my mind had to say about it. It didn't matter what Gabe had done, I still found myself missing him.

"I guess so," I said, between sobs. "Who needs him?"

After a few more minutes of crying, I finally pulled away from Cora's shoulder. My tears had left a giant wet spot on the upper part of her shirt.

"I'm going to give you a choice," Cora said. "There are a few things we can do that will make you feel better. I'll let you decide which."

I chuckled and wiped my cheeks with my sleeve. "Okay. Hit me."

"The way I see it, the only real way to get through this initial heartbreak is by using humor, booze or throwing yourself into your work. So we can either go do something that will make us laugh, go get drunk, or work on the blog."

The blog... I thought.

It made me think of Gabe and how upset he was at me for blogging about our dates. Still, though, I refused to let myself feel guilty about it. What I had done was entirely different and not nearly as extreme. I had never even used Gabe's full name in my writing. None of my readers actually knew who he was. They just saw that I was dating some guy named Gabe who I happened to really like. But what *he* had done to me, with the ads... it was far worse. My full name, picture and my blog was being used without my permission.

"Well, what are you thinking?" Cora said. "I gave you some options. Which do you want to do?"

"You mentioned booze in your list of choices, but I'm just afraid that there's not enough alcohol in Orlando to get me through this one," I said.

"Oh, I beg to differ," Cora replied. "I just recently stocked up my liquor cabinet."

Then she sat up on the lounge chair, placing her hands onto my shoulders. Her lips curled up into a smile and her eyes widened.

"I have an idea," she said, with excitement.

Uh oh, I thought with a little trepidation. This could either be really bad or really good. Although, regardless, it was sure to be interesting. Any idea of Cora's would be crazy enough to be fun.

"What is it?" I asked, almost afraid of the answer.

"Disney World," she stated, as matter-of-factly as if she had told me the sky was blue.

"Disney World?"

"Yes, Disney World. Disney World, Harper!" She shook my shoulders and made my head wobble. "That's how we're going to get you over this. It's preposterous to sit here and cry it out. We both know that's not going to help. So now I'm making the executive decision to take us to the place where dreams are born. We're getting drunk at Disney World. Put *that* on your blog when you tell everyone about the break-up."

I couldn't help but to laugh, yet also agree, that it was probably the best idea I had heard in a while.

"Okay, let's do it," I said, with a nod. "Yeah, this could be fun. Let's go to Disney World."

"Yes!" Cora squealed, as she hopped up and ran to her bedroom. "Let's pick out some cute outfits to wear. This is going to be amazing!"

I gave Jack a few more pets before setting him on the floor. Then I got up to meet Cora in her room to decide on what to wear for the day trip that was ahead of us.

God, this sucks, I thought as I tried to plaster a happy smile on my face. *It hurts, it hurts, it hurts.* My heart ached so badly. It even hurt to laugh, but I guessed it felt better than crying. Plus maybe Cora was right. Maybe some carefree fun at the happiest place on earth will rub off and make me happy.

It certainly couldn't hurt to try.

CHAPTER 22

> *Well, the time has come. Every beginning has an end, and my relationship has found its end. Two weeks ago, Mr. Perfect Match and I broke up and it is time for the corresponding blog post (because blogging about breakups is the best way to move on, right??)*
>
> *It's not the typical kind of post I'm used to writing. My life is filled with many more bad dates than bad breakups, and maybe that's a good thing. But it also means that I'm entering new territory without the right map to guide me. They say it's better to have loved and lost than never to have loved*

I STOPPED WRITING and glared at the screen. I highlighted the last sentence and hit delete as if the force of my click would hurt the words as they left the page. *Love.* It was like a bad word, something I had been conditioned not to say. And

Gabe deserved no exception, even if it would appease an old stupid cliché about breakups.

After a few moments of contemplation I picked up again where I left off.

> *Time is a weird thing. It has the ability to pass in the blink of an eye, or as a small flame that grows slowly in size until finally it has engulfed everything in its path. I guess heartbreaks are like small fires in your chest. And fire hurts.*
>
> *Two weeks has done little to ease the pain, and I guess that's to be expected. But friends help too. And when you have good friends you show up to their house after a breakup and they take you to get drunk at Disney World.*
>
> *And then you get back from Disney World and you're hung-over and you remember why you had to go in the first place and you're sad and you cry and Mickey Mouse isn't there to wipe your tears.*
>
> *So then you go to your blog. And it's time I caught you all up anyway. So this post is about a relationship that ended badly with someone who only anticipates ever having bad dates anyway. Go figure.*

I PAUSED AGAIN. I had been drafting the post in my head for weeks now. I knew it would suck to actually write, but it was going better than I had anticipated. Writing had always been like a type of therapy for me. It allowed me the chance to unwind and exhale and create something beautiful out of something awful. It was no wonder I made a living off of documenting my bad dates, it had always felt natural. Some people have their diary, I had my blog.

But it was tricky nonetheless. I still had too much emotion to accurately convey in writing. I was looking for the best way to detail the aftermath of our breakup without sounding like I was throwing myself my own personal pity-party. No one would want to read that.

I had even pulled up the six stages of grief, which felt a little excessive, to look for some sort of guidance. Shock, denial, anger, bargaining, depression and acceptance, it said.

Shock seemed appropriate. Boy, was I shocked. But then I think I jumped straight to anger and then to depression. *Harper's 3 stages of grief,* I thought. *We'll see if I ever make it to acceptance.*

I decided to include the stages of grief anyway, at least as a way to relate to my readers who were surely familiar with the concept, even if it was total bogus.

Don't laugh at me, but I actually looked up the six stages of grief. They say that first you're shocked, and then you progress through denial, anger, bargaining, depression and then finally onto acceptance. I think any of us who have had a relationship end because of dishonesty have felt a level of shock, perhaps even denial. Which is a sad thing in the context of a relationship, and it naturally leads to anger.

But I think that what's important, though, is to reflect on the relationship, the good and the bad. Heartbreak sucks and I've certainly had my fair share of booze and ice cream, but I'm glad it *happened. This relationship reminded me that good dates **are** possible, and good, dateable people actually do exist.*

*They're out there, wandering around somewhere. They're at their day jobs, at the gym, at the park. I know sometimes it can feel like a game of Where's Waldo, and sometimes you just want to light the page on fire and burn all the useless faces used to camouflage Waldo in a sea of chaos. But you just have to remember that Waldo **is** there, he's just hidden. Not every guy is a bundled-up package of confused intents and irrational impulses. I don't think so anyway...*

No, there are good guys out there, they just take some searching. Or even still, sometimes you'll stumble on them. Sometimes something weird and awkward will turn into a lovely friendship between two unassuming people, and that's the thing about life I guess.

*I'm starting to feel like I'm almost ready to jump back into the wild and treacherous jungle that is 'dating.' I must share a rule with you all and if you're a longtime reader you may have seen it in past posts, but my policy is that you must always allow yourself **half** the time of your previous relationship before seeking a rebound. I'll do the math for everyone, because this is a blog post not an algebra class. I have another two weeks until I'm allowed to get back at it. Which feels right, I guess.*

I PAUSED AGAIN, this time just to exhale and collect my thoughts. I was happy with the post so far and it was almost starting to write itself, a feeling that usually accompanied my better pieces.

The drafted idea for the post that had been building in my head was fostered with far more hate than the post that was actually coming out, which was probably a good thing. My readers wouldn't want a pity-party *or* an angry rant. Still, I worked with an inventory of ideas that had culminated through many hours of crying, talking to Rosie and Cora and binge watching Netflix. They were combining nicely with the ideas that came to me as I typed.

I had certainly envisioned much more bashing and criticism, but it didn't seem to belong. *I guess I can bash that stupid website now,* I thought. Oddly, it was the first time it had occurred to me. Blogging about Kindling Dating was the first thing I had wanted to do when Rosie first thrust the commitment on me, but now it felt monotonous. Ironically it wasn't the website that had failed me, it was Gabe.

Part of me wanted to attack the way he had hid the news until eventually I found it on my own accord. Part of me wanted to call him elaborate names that my readers would find funny, but I couldn't.

I looked up at the clock hanging above my desk. It was getting late.

My eyes looked over the words sitting motionless on the screen until I came upon the blinking curser at the bottom of the page, then I read it again.

Some blogs I wrote were several pages long, some merely filled a single screen. I was strict to not force a word count on myself but rather allow the posts to come naturally. Some dates genuinely required several pages in order to divulge the entire disaster. Others needed no more than a few details and a quick physical description to make you cringe. I had learned that it's not always about *how much* you say but *what you say*, and I followed the principle religiously. The popularity of my posts wasn't dependent on length and this post would be one of my shorter ones, which was okay.

It would also be much more sentimental than usual. My readers weren't used to having me gush at them with sappy expressions of blues and heartbreak. They were much more accustomed to sarcastic tirades about failed dates. But this was a different kind of failure.

Still the post seemed to have a positive quality about it and I felt like it would be received well. Sometimes I felt like I knew my readers, what they liked, disliked, wanted to read and what they thought was funny. Their comments were always entertaining and allowed for a sort of connection.

I began again with my readers in mind.

> *How many of you have been derailed by a breakup? I spend so much time on here talking about bad dates that I was naive to the fact that sometimes your last date can be worse than the first one ever could be, am I right??*
>
> *But that's life, and life is about resilience. I have bounced back from too many bad dates to allow one punch in the face to knock me out. I am a boxer who can get back up. I can take another round.*
>
> *The last two months have taught me that bad dates earned their name because good dates exist. If all dates were the same as what I describe on here, than we would call them all 'dates' and we*

wouldn't distinguish between good and bad and I wouldn't have a blog to illustrate the absurdities that we've all dealt with.

So instead, we have dates that all fall somewhere between the good, the bad and the ugly. I guess it might be time to start thinking about exploring again and get back to blogging regularly. You all are wonderful and I've missed you guys!

And before I finish up I want to send a special THANK YOU shout out everyone that submitted a bad date story in the last two months. I know it's not easy to write about such a topic, but I received some truly fantastic and entertaining submissions —more than I was able to post, so I want to thank you all!

Everyone stay at it and don't get discouraged by a few halfwits and Gloomy Garys here and there. And when you have that breakup that seems to knock you off your rocker: drink a few margaritas (with extra salt), rent a couple corny, syrupy romance movies, have some ice cream, go buy some wine and get back on your feet!

Oh... and read my blog if you need some clueless oaf to laugh at for a moment.

But most of all, don't forget that you're all wonderful.

Thanks for reading and comment below on your special remedy that got you through your worst break up.

Bye for now!

I CLICKED enter and then took a second to lean back and smile at the post. It really did feel good to finally flush it out and release some of the built up angst that had sat like a cloud in my head for the last two weeks. I felt like I had lost weight through writing the post. I felt lighter.

I knew that some of the post hadn't quite been a *lie,* but was slightly exaggerated. It helped though. Forcing out some positivity in conjunction with the breakup was good and I hoped that it would only help me to move on. If I told my readers that I was a boxer who could stand up after a punch, than I was *going* to stand back up.

I looked at the clock again and hit Publish.

I fled to the kitchen to make some tea and then returned to my post. I didn't often sit to watch the site's dashboard blow up. Usually I went to bed and returned in the morning to the array of comments. Tonight, however, I did. In the few minutes that I had been gone, my social media was already starting to react. My Twitter and Tumblr were racking up hits and comments were beginning to accumulate below the blog.

Sometimes I felt a little narcissistic as I took in my readers' feedback. But then I remembered that I was a writer and I made my living off of entertaining other people. Their entertainment was my fuel and their feedback was rewarding. *And there's nothing wrong with accepting a few nice compliments, especially after you've had your heart crushed,* I thought.

Getting back to my blog and my readers would be crucial in moving forward. Gabe could break my heart, but he couldn't break me as a writer. I was still good at what I did I reminded myself as I scrolled through the comments. All I could really do now was take each day at a time and hope that what I told my readers would actually start to manifest itself in real life.

took a break from watching my blog to make some belated dinner. I heated up some left over lasagna and made a milkshake with some of the ice cream still left in the fridge as post-breakup comfort food. I couldn't help but make fun of myself and my current state of affairs. It felt only fitting to throw on an episode of Grey's Anatomy on Netflix.

After about a half hour I heard the phone ring.

Immediately my heart skipped a beat. I had posted my blog late at night and had done so purposefully to avoid an instant reaction from Rosie or my Mom. But with as late as it was, realistically they were the only ones that would be calling.

I checked the caller I.D. on the phone before answering. It was Rosie, which was better than Mom. I took a deep breath and clicked to accept the call.

"Hey, Rosie," I attempted cheerfully.

"Hey, Big Sis!" she exclaimed.

"What are you doing up so late?" I asked.

"I fell asleep kind of early, and then the baby woke me

up. My sleep schedule is so crazy now, this little guy dictates every second that I'm awake or sleeping," she explained. "But anyway, I just fed him and got him back to bed and I read your post and wanted to call and talk. I knew you'd be up."

Rosie had her baby almost immediately after the breakup, which was awful timing for me. I had just gotten back from Orlando when she had gone into labor and I rushed to the hospital to meet them. The breakup had drastically marred the occasion for me. Interacting with my mother hadn't helped. But with everyone so enthralled with the new baby I was able to dodge some relationship interrogation and had done my best to put on a mask and hide my sorrow.

"Oh, okay," I said. "What'd you think?"

I braced myself for the inevitable pity and judgment that was coming.

"Harper, your post was so good! I don't think I've ever seen you write like that! I had no idea you could be so..." she paused as hesitation hung in her voice, "...so deep and sentimental with your posts."

"I guess I'll take that as a compliment." I forced a small giggle. "Thanks Sis."

"It is a compliment," she assured me. "It was really good," she paused again. "Still, it made me a little sad."

Here we go, I thought. *I'm the one that's supposed to be sad, not you.*

"You shouldn't be sad Rosie," I told her. "It was a post about new beginnings."

"Yeah, but are you sure you're ready for new beginnings?" she asked carefully.

"I'm positive," I lied.

"I just..." she began but I interrupted. I could already sense my frustration beginning to build.

"Look, that site and all the algorithms and everything were wrong," I told her. "Gabe and I didn't fit. It's the same as any other dating site, it's just a scam."

"It's not a scam!" she protested and I could hear her dejected sentiments seeping through. "It just didn't work this time."

"Okay, it's not a scam, but my profile and my information just wasn't really right for their matching formulas or whatever," I said but quickly added, "I'm not saying it's your fault."

"It sounds a little like you are. Harper, I answered all of those questions based only on you. Maybe it's not exactly how you would have answered, but it's how people see you." Her words were firm and rigid.

"Right, I know-" I started, but it was her turn to interrupt me.

"-I even had Thomas' confirmation on all of it," she told me, heat rising in her voice. "We answered all the questions as if we were talking to someone about you."

"Rosie, I read through all your answers and your conversation with him. It was a really good effort, but it's just not how I would have answered that stuff or how I would have flirted with him," I told her gently. "It just happened to work well enough to land a first date."

"Yeah, a first date that blossomed pretty damn quickly!" she piped.

"And ended pretty damn quickly too," I piped back. I rubbed the bridge of my nose with my fingers, trying to stop the headache I knew was coming. "Look, I really do appreciate your intentions with all this but it's time to recognize that it didn't really work out. That's just how it goes."

"Harper, even if you don't agree with me I still created you a profile that was good enough to land you a date with the *first guy* that you've actually liked. What's wrong with that?" she asked. "And I know you want to argue with everything I've said, but maybe it just takes a little perspective. You're always so hard on yourself Harper, it's probably why your such an amazing writer but it's also why you're a bad first dater."

I laughed, but it was mostly out of frustration. *Yeah, thanks Sis, that's exactly what I needed to hear right now,* I thought. The argument was getting harder to fight. Part of me was mad at my sister for being so good at reading between the lines of my breakup. She *had* landed me the best guy I could remember meeting a very long time. I couldn't dispute that.

"I'm sorry about what happened. But I also *really* think you should give him another chance," she said. "Crappy things happen in relationships but the good and strong ones work through them. Who's to say this isn't something that you guys can work past?"

"It's over, Rosie. It's done. He's not trying to get in touch with me and I'm certainly not trying to get in touch with him."

I heard Rosie sigh into the phone so I continued. "I'm just trying to get over this as quickly as possible. And we weren't even together that long! I'm just going to try and get back to my blog and my normal life and stuff."

"By your blog, you mean more bad dates," she said cynically.

"Come on Rosie. What am I supposed to do? Stop working and stop paying rent? That'll solve a lot of things," I said, not minding as my defensive sarcasm came out.

The truth was that I wasn't even really sure that I was ready for more bad dates; in fact I knew I wasn't. She was right, I'd never been with anyone that felt as *right* as Gabe. I wanted to give in and cry and tell her how much I missed him and how it felt weirdly like I had lost a longtime friend. But it all seemed silly. We had only been together for two months. Two months is a fraction of the time that it takes to plan a wedding. *For God's sake, Rosie had carried a baby in her stomach for nine months. Gabe and I didn't even make it through the first trimester,* I thought and almost made a similar comment but Rosie spoke up first.

"Or maybe, you should come hang out with your sister and your new baby nephew," she offered. "Tommy is just growing like a weed. I'm sure he's put on a full inch since you saw him last."

"In just a week?" I asked with a genuine delight. I was extremely thankful that she had shifted the subject. "How is my favorite man?"

"Oh, he's good! He slept for a whole three hours last night," she said in the proud voice that only a new mother could achieve.

"I can't wait to see him again," I said and a smile filled my face as I imagined the new baby growing and taking in the world around him.

Since Tommy's birth, Rosie had already sent hundreds of pictures to the family group. Consequently, I was also forced to field my Mother's comments that always seemed to contain a condescending hint aimed in my direction. But I was glad to receive the pictures and I beamed every time I saw the baby's bright blue eyes cushioned between his two plump cheeks. His grin was still a half smiled dominated by drool, but it was beyond adorable.

"Tomorrow Thomas and I are going to take him for a

little photo shoot," she said. "I want to get them done before he gets too big."

"Oh, that'll be fun," I said. "What are you planning on doing?"

"We're both going to wear these white shirts and Tommy's going to wear this little sailor onesie outfit I found the other day." Her happy smile shone through her voice. "It makes him look so cute."

"As if he needs a costume to make him look cute," I said, just appreciating chatting casually about her baby instead of my dating life. It made things feel normal.

She laughed, "Yeah, I guess that's true. I have the cutest baby in the world!"

"Will you make sure to send me a copy of the pictures when you get them?" I asked. "I have a spot on my desk that could use a nice framed copy."

"You got it," she promised. "I'm always happy to send more pictures, you should know that by now."

"I'm always happy to get them," I said. "He is my current screen saver and phone wallpaper."

"And really, you need to come over and visit soon," she scolded. "I'm determined for his first words to be 'Mommy,' but if you try hard enough maybe you can teach him your name early on, that'd be cute!"

"Harp-y," I said, trying my best to say it in baby-speak. "Kind of sounds like herpes..."

We both laughed. "Maybe we should just call you 'auntie' or something," she offered.

"I'd like that," I told her. "I'm going to go eat my dinner, so you have fun tomorrow, enjoy your photo shoot and say hi to Thomas and baby Tommy for me." I hoped to end the conversation without allowing it to slip back into the hallow pit of darkness that had become my romantic life.

"I will. And Harper," she paused and I knew exactly where she was about to go. I would be foolish to think I had escaped all together. "You know Mom's going to read this post soon, too."

"So you mean while you're posing and having someone take cute pictures of you and your baby, I'm going to have to try and survive a barrage of Mom's drone strikes?" I scrunched up my face thinking about it. "I might not be alive next time you call."

Rosie faked a sympathetic laugh. "You know, she only wants you to be happy with someone."

"We both know she's going to gloss over every motivational word I wrote about resilience and yell at me for ruining a 'good' relationship." I sighed, but there was nothing to do about it. "It'll be fine, I guess. I'll just tell her what she wants to hear."

"I would leave out the part about lining up more dates," she teased.

"Thanks Rosie. I'll do that," I said, rolling my eyes.

"You know I love you! And so does Mom," she said. "We both just want you to be happy and you seemed so happy with Gabe."

I hated to hear her say his name. It felt like treason. I desperately wanted to end the conversation but I couldn't help myself.

"And so what if my *real* perfect guy is waiting in one of the dates I lined up?" I asked. "Don't they always say you need to get rid of the negative things in order to make room for something better?"

"I guess. As long as you have the mindset that something better *can* come along," she insisted. "Instead of just more terrible dates for your blog."

"You know me Rosie, I've got my eyes peeled," I said.

"Mmm, hmm," she hummed dryly. "Well I guess that's enough of a lecture for tonight. I really did like your post tonight, though. It was really well written."

"Thanks, Rosie," I said, taking the compliment. "I love you."

"I love you too," she said. "Talk soon?"

"Of course," I promised. "Give that nephew of mine a big kiss for me."

"I will. Bye bye," she said. I echoed her farewell but she had already ended the call.

I took a breath as if I had just finished some sort of marathon. The phone call had genuinely exhausted me. *Ironic the way she could praise and lecture me at the same time*, I thought. *Then again, she learned from the best.*

I knew my Mother's interrogation would be far worse and much more intense. She had been the biggest fan of my relationship with Gabe and had been deeply saddened when I called to tell her about the breakup. Though she was sad in a different way; instead of words of condolence she was almost frustrated that things hadn't worked out.

She had called after every post I had written about my relationship with Gabe and I had appreciated the opportunity to bathe in her approval. Tomorrow's phone call would be much different.

Maybe I should be prepared with another guy that came along during my time of despair to sweep me off my feet, I thought jokingly. *She would like the sound of that. And my readers would probably eat that up.* Even they had appreciated my posts about Gabe. They had seemed to enjoy the switch up.

Or perhaps they had enjoyed a bit of continuity. I had never lied outright to readers before—just fudged the details to protect the guilty party—but I'd also never been completely immobilized by a heartbreak. I had no idea how I was going to go out on another date anytime soon.

I knew I wasn't ready to get back on the dating carousel as much as I knew I had lied to Rosie about the possibility of the 'perfect guy' lying in wait. I hated to think that she might have been even a little bit right about the connection I had felt. The idea of replacing Gabe was daunting and impossible. *But maybe not in the world of cyberspace,* I thought. The Internet was open to whatever clever spark of witty narration I could throw at it. And if my readers—and my Mother —demanded continuity, I could give them continuity.

CHAPTER 24

sat down at my computer and clicked on the Internet. It was always the first step in starting a new blog post and I could almost feel the writer's block start to set in as a blank window popped up on the screen and began loading.

It had been just over two months since the breakup and about a month and a half since I had introduced Brian.

Brian was a tall guy with a toned body, dark hair and eyes bluer than an open sky on a summer's day. He was funny, smart, a hard worker in his career as a physical trainer, a huge sports fan and… completely fake.

I had decided to create Brian in order to appease my Mother and to use as a marketing tool for the blog. After my readers had obsessed over my relationship with Gabe, Brian was designed to be Gabe 2.0 and to carry the burden of a new and passionate relationship. And completely fabricating a fake relationship was *much* easier than actually getting consumed by one.

Brian took me on elaborate dates to all the exciting places around town without ever a boring moment. His father had a boat that was perfect for evenings on the water. He was a great cook and had gone to culinary school before shifting his passion to physical training. He had even gotten me into exercising and we liked to take runs on the beach. It was amazing how easy a relationship could be when you dictated every single thing about it.

And already Brian had been a huge sell for the blog. My readers loved him, and it was hard not to. I had created him that way. Every post brought in more hits than the last and I had even gained readers since his introduction.

Part of its success was the work of Cora, who had assumed the duty of using Kindling Dating to go on dates as fodder for the blog. I didn't want to completely scrap the concept that had made the site what it was, and Cora was more than willing to do the dirty work. We called it "Tactless Tuesday".

Between Brian and "Tactless Tuesday," The blog was booming.

Initially, I was a little surprised. Cora's stories were entertaining, well written and extremely hilarious. She was already a sarcastic person and the notion of ranting about guys came to her like water to a fish. She had already gone on numerous dates and had passed on her anecdotes to be used as consistent filler for the blog. As if the model of dating as an assignment wasn't already enough, Cora was hooked the second she saw the feedback from her first Tactless Tuesday post. My readers loved her.

I had also continued to accept reader submissions for 'Worst Wednesday,' which had developed a small popularity of its own. Occasionally, I came across a submission that seemed obnoxiously fake. There were certain things that made for pretty obvious clues. I'd laugh, and I never posted one that seemed *too* phony, but the irony occasionally caused me to stop and think; was I not guilty of the same thing?

Perhaps I was just better at concealing my crime.

But my crime of lying about dates had made a positive impact all around. Mom couldn't be happier that I was in a new 'happy relationship' with a great guy. Rosie had reluctantly promised not to spill the secret to Mom, though with her new baby she was usually too exhausted to even threaten the possibility. Cora was enjoying her new role, and my readers continued to voice their compliments on the site.

All was well. Except me. I was not well at all.

I was still miserable and my memories with Gabe were like the relentless clouds of a storm. Everyday came a sort of rain that was inescapable, no matter how hard I tried. I no longer bothered Cora with my depressing outbursts and I had lost Rosie as an outlet as soon as I invented Brian instead of trying to fix things with Gabe.

How can I still be this upset. How can I still be upset after a period of time that was almost longer than we had dated for? I thought. *Is this what heartbreak is like? How many more bottles of wine do I need?*

I started to wonder if the 'relationship' I had invented with Brian was more about compensating for the void that Gabe had left. But I rejected the idea quickly. *I'm not a therapist,* I thought, *and I'm not going to start psychoanalyzing myself now. Or my blog.*

Besides, it was just a blog and my tactics were becoming tremendously successful.

I had been sitting blankly in front of my computer for several minutes before the chaotic spiral of my thoughts had reminded me that it was time to work. The blog needed a new post, and more than that, it needed a new spark. Making up fake dates was kind of fun at first, but it was getting old. I needed something fresh, something riveting, some sort of twist.

Where am I even going with this, I thought and then said aloud to myself. *Sure, I can give it another spark, but how am I going to get out of this mess?* The thought was heavy in my head. I was deep and I knew it. I had hinted more and more that things between 'Brian' and I were getting serious. *How am I ever going to end this?*

But beside the challenge of completely terminating an intense relationship on the blog, there was no answer for breaking the news to my mother. I knew I could completely end it online and maybe even use its ending beneficially for the blog, but there was no way I could tell my Mother that my entire relationship had been one big lie. She was already demanding to meet him, and had been for weeks. Luckily, Brian was a busy guy who was constantly trying to make room for me in his schedule. Rosie had also helped to assure Mom that all was well and Brian was a tremendous guy who was simply very busy. I had been able to stay afloat this long, but I knew that the water was rising.

Maybe I'll get hit by lighting during the next gulf storm or something, I thought. *That way I'll get a free pass out of this mess.* I decided that was probably the best-case scenario.

I became frustrated as I looked back at my computer and realized I had gotten absolutely no work done in the past half hour. Time was ticking. Cora was in town in Miami for a business conference. She was desperately hoping for a promotion to escape the grind of trying to fill shifts and maintain staffing. We had planned to meet for dinner later that night, and I had expected to use the day to write up a new post about Brian.

"Where am I going with this," I whispered aloud once more. "What are we doing next? Huh Brian?" I was beginning to talk anxiously to the computer screen. "What else do you have in store?"

I sat for a few more moments as I attempted to answer the questions for myself. *You're a sweet guy and things are starting to get serious,* I thought, tapping my finger restlessly on the desk. *Maybe it's time for you to take things to the next level?*

Sometimes as a writer, you use details that seem to be readily available, and my dinner with Cora was the perfect chance.

"Maybe it's time for you to propose?" I murmured the words ominously and then began typing.

> *Have you ever gotten a call that seemed to be wired with an electric excitement? As if a sort of energy was transferred through the phone line with soft spoken words as its vehicle?*
>
> *I have that feeling. I have a big feeling. I have a feeling that tonight might be **the night**.*
>
> *Things with Brian have been going really well. Not a day goes by that I don't feel like I'm still falling head over heels in love with this guy. He has continuously spoiled me and I spend every day on cloud nine in a dreamy state of bliss. Sometimes I make myself sick with my own sappy feelings, but I guess that's falling in love, and I'm okay with it for now.*
>
> *I want to take a moment to pause and reflect, just for a quick second. I want to reflect on life and all its crazy ups and downs.*
>
> *Just over two months ago, as you all know, I went through a pretty bad breakup. I dated a guy*

that I actually really liked, and I had my heart broken when our dynamics turned into a dishonest mess.

I PAUSED and reread the last few sentences I had just finished typing. As I wrote every post I wondered whether or not Gabe would read it. My blog had been a partial reason for our breakup and I wondered if he remembered it with more anger or curiosity. I wondered if he had ever been inclined to sneak a peek, searching for an indication on how I had moved on. I wondered if he knew about Brian.

Probably not, I thought in a way that forcefully derailed my train of thought. *Why would he? I wouldn't if I were him.*

Still, I sat with the idea for a moment longer. I wanted to think he was reading; I wanted to think he *had* been reading. It was part of the reason that Brian was such an amazing cook. I wanted to think that he looked on the blog with a sort of nostalgic jealousy. Mostly I wanted to know that he was hurting like I was.

I slowly forced my attention back to the screen in front of me. If there was *any* chance that he was reading at all, I was going to make it count, and I picked up where I left off.

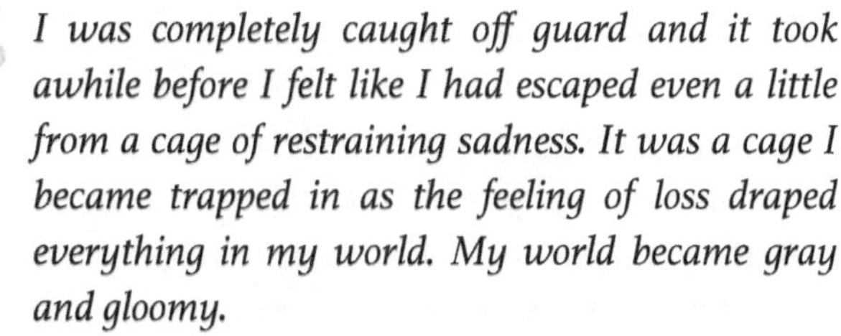

I was completely caught off guard and it took awhile before I felt like I had escaped even a little from a cage of restraining sadness. It was a cage I became trapped in as the feeling of loss draped everything in my world. My world became gray and gloomy.

But then came Brian, and day-by-day I began

*to see things repaint themselves and return to their colorful splendor as my world was reinvented. Life is a highway, and life is a beach and life is precious and it's all the innumerable clichés that people have discovered and cemented throughout the years. But most of all, life is **crazy**. Life is full of more twists and turns than we can ever imagine and when they become apparent or obvious, they're still just as shocking as before.*

Two months ago and right after a brutal breakup, I would have never imagined I'd be in another relationship that's even better. Sometimes you've got to get rid of the negative to make room for something far bigger and better.

I ALMOST DELETED my last sentence, but I decided against it. I had just used the same phrase in conversation with Rosie and I employed it again as a bit of a shout-out, though I knew she wouldn't *really* like that I had made light of my lie in such a way.

But if I was going to use and commit to this Brain thing, then I was going to do so entirely.

I'm just lucky that my 'bigger and better' came around quickly. Brian is a blessing that I am thankful for everyday.

This morning he called—that kind of call that's pulsing with electric excitement—and asked if I wanted to go to dinner at my favorite fancy restaurant in downtown Miami. I said that of course I want to go! So we now have a dinner date scheduled tonight.

Most of you will remember that Brian lives in the kitchen the way a bumblebee occupies its hive; he genuinely likes to cook up a nice homemade dinner.

*Certainly, we like to go out on occasion and he's got a knack for finding the **good** spots. But when he recommends going out to my **favorite** restaurant...well... it's a good sign. It's a sign that there might just be a shiny pearl in this oyster's shell. It's a sign that should be considered in conjunction with all the other good signs in our relationship. It's a sign that, if I was a rational person with a coherent line of thinking, I would think is an indication that he might... dare I say it... propose?*

I WONDERED how an outright lie could sound so whimsically romantic. It was just one of the many enigmas of life, I decided. Something I didn't need to decipher in that moment. There's too many ironies in life, like the fact that I would be going out to dinner with my best friend instead of a dreamy guy who's about to get down on one knee and propose. But that didn't stop me from running with it. I liked how the post was coming together. I knew my readers were going to absolutely eat it up and I wanted to give them as big a dose as I could.

I was forced to stop and laugh for a moment. *Anonymity is a beautiful thing,* I thought. I was fabricating a massive fib and if there were any reader out there looking to steal a peek into the life of my alter ego, they would be looking for a happy couple gawking soppily at each other, not two lunatic friends obnoxiously talking at a level that was slightly above their surrounding compatriots. *I might even deserve a trophy for this one,* I thought before returning to work.

I thought I was the girl that goes out on bad dates, not the girl that gets proposed to (though maybe I should stop jinxing myself before I even get there).

No, but I really do have a good feeling about this one. I have such a good feeling that I'm going to have to be careful not to drop a hint of my own! I'll probably sit there tapping my foot through the whole night. But I don't even know if all this anticipation can keep me from being surprised and ecstatic when it does happen for real. I'll probably blush until my face becomes so flush and purple that he considers revoking the proposal. But I'll be sure to say 'yes' and jump in his arms before he has the chance, fear not.

So, I apologize for the short post, but I wanted reach out before the big moment. I'm pretty sure it's coming tonight, and I want everyone to cross their fingers for me.

Thank you all for reading! Comment below if you have a memorable proposal story!

Hopefully the next time I post, it will be with exciting news!

Bye for now!

I TOOK a punctuating breath in the same way that I always did upon finishing a new post. My eyes glossed over the ending and I cringed as I reread the words *next time I post.* The thought of my next post made me tense and I noticed I had clinched my hands into fists.

I had no idea what my next post was going to be. None. I couldn't lie to my mother about a proposal, but I didn't want Brian to break up with me, either.

I purposefully relaxed and exhaled out through my nose. The post was done, and that was that. Any sort of resolution for the situation was not going to magically appear, no matter how much I wanted one to.

This is good for now, I thought. *This will be a popular post and then whatever happens, happens. Maybe everything will end up solving itself. That's a thing, right?*

I sat quietly for a few minutes without even doing much thinking until the sound of my watch alarm woke me from my daze. It was time to get ready for dinner. If I was actually getting ready for a dinner with a possible proposal, I probably would have left myself more than twenty minutes for the process. But instead I changed into clothes fit for an evening in Miami and threw on a pair of heels. There wasn't going to be a proposal, but we were still going to my favorite spot, an upscale Italian restaurant with the best garlic bread in all of Miami. The location was so conveniently close to the hotel where Cora was staying that I couldn't resist.

I was getting excited and had begun to mull over exactly how I was going to tell Cora that right before I left I had posted a blog about how I expected to be proposed to at our dinner. With the absurdity still on my mind I grabbed my purse, fished out my keys and dashed out the door.

CHAPTER 25

"So all of your readers think you're out with Brian right now?" Cora asked.

I nodded. "Yep, I've duped them all into thinking Brian is a real person that loves me just the way I should be loved. It's too bad I had to make all that up, though, isn't it."

"Whatever. I think it's fine." Cora just shrugged. "But I have to ask you an important question, Harper."

"What is it?" I asked, a little nervous.

Cora turned to the side and set her jaw, making a serious face. "Do I look like a Brian to you?"

I busted out laughing. Her goofy antics got me every time.

"You know, you actually do!" I exclaimed. "You make a perfect Brian! Wow, I'm one lucky girl to be on a date with such a handsome man."

"Aw, thanks!" she said, as she turned back to face me and grinned. "If I talk like this does it make me sound like a Brian, too?"

She lowered her voice as much as possible and crinkled her eyebrows together. I was laughing so hard that tears were streaming down my face. The good kind of tears, though, not the ones that I had had for weeks after my breakup with Gabe.

It's kind of funny that Cora is a better date than most of the men I've been out with, I thought. *At least she can keep me laughing.*

The waiter strolled up and set a small plate of tiramisu in front of us. Cora and I picked up our forks and began to nibble on it.

"This is my favorite thing in the entire world," I said, as I licked my fork clean. I tried not to think of the tiramisu I'd had with Gabe.

"It's good, but I can probably think of a few others things that I like more than this," Cora replied. "Like coffee and martinis. Just to name a couple."

"Good point," I agreed. "But this is right up there in the top three."

The dessert was gobbled up within a few minutes and I sat back, gently patting my belly. "I'm stuffed."

"Me too," Cora agreed.

"Should I ask for the check?" I asked. This dinner was going to be my treat since she was doing so much to help me with the blog, but I knew Cora would at least try and split it with me.

"Yeah, get the check when you see the waiter again," she said, setting her napkin down on the table. "I'm going to run and use the bathroom really quickly before we leave."

"Sounds good," I told her, stealing the last bite of tiramisu.

Cora hopped up from her chair and weaved through the other tables in the restaurant, making her way to the bathrooms. I chuckled to myself. For some reason, I thought about the date with what's-his-name, where he stayed in the bathroom for twenty minutes until he knew that I had paid our tab. Of course, Cora would never do such a thing, but the memory of that date had me laughing to myself.

Things could be worse, I thought. *I could have ended up with that guy. Or worse yet, what if I had ended up with the "professional bowler"? God, I'd be sitting in a bowling alley right now just hating my life and trying to drink as much beer as possible from those little plastic cups just to ease the pain.*

The waiter walked up, pulling my attention away from my thoughts.

"Can I get you anything else this evening?" he asked.

"Oh, I think we're good," I replied. "We'll take our check whenever you get a chance."

"Of course. I'll be back in a moment."

The waiter disappeared around the corner. As I waited, I casually leaned back in my chair, looking at my nails.

I really need to get a mani-pedi sometime soon. It's been too long since I've spoiled myself. It's definitely time for some of that.

When I looked back up, I noticed the waiter had already dropped the check off on the table. I reached for my purse to grab my card to pay for the meal.

Cora's helped me so much over the past couple of months with getting over Gabe, that a nice dinner is the least I can do.

My attention suddenly lifted to the front part of the restaurant, where the wooden hostess podium was located. I saw a man standing there, speaking to the young lady who worked for the restaurant. I squinted when I saw the man and then rubbed my eyes with the back of my hand.

I must be seeing things, I thought. *I mean, this isn't the first time I think I've seen him somewhere.*

When I looked back up, though, I knew that I wasn't hallucinating. Gabe, the man who had taken my heart and then broken it, was standing at the front of the restaurant.

He was wearing a black suit with a white undershirt. He looked frantic, as he moved his hands around while speaking to the hostess.

I didn't even know what to think. I felt a rush of adrenaline fill me and all I could do was try not to fall out of my chair from shock. I watched as he spoke to the hostess, who turned and pointed toward me. Immediately, Gabe pivoted his head and for the first time since I had left his house in anger two months prior, our eyes met.

"What's he doing here?" I whispered to myself.

As soon as he saw me, Gabe marched past the hostess and made his way straight toward my table. He looked furious, or was it frightened? I couldn't tell. But he was walking quickly, making large strides as he maneuvered between the other restaurant patrons.

My heart began to pound so loudly that I could hear the blood whooshing behind my eardrums. It almost felt like I was outside of my body, watching as he approach me. It was as though it was happening to someone else, maybe someone on TV, for a reality show or something. It just didn't make any sense. I had a hard time believing that what I was seeing was real.

Within seconds, Gabe was standing next to me. He was breathing hard and there was a little sweat on his forehead. It looked like he must have been running to get to the restaurant.

"Harper." My name came out in a rush.

I was completely shocked. So much so, that my brain couldn't even get any words out to my lips.

"Harper, I've spent the last two months in my house, hating myself. I've been so mad and so embarrassed about what happened that I couldn't face anybody," he explained. His eyes never left my face. "But then I read the blog post that you put up tonight. I wasn't going to show my face again, but when I saw that you thought Brian was going to propose to you, I had to come here to stop him. I can't let you go through with it. I don't want you to marry him."

As Gabe spoke, I realized that I hadn't moved a single inch since he had approached. I was completely frozen, unable to do anything but listen.

"I can't live without you, Harper. You're the best thing that's ever happened to me," he announced. The words seemed to be spilling from him like water from a well. "I know I screwed up. I screwed up bad. I should have told you about what I did for a living. There was no real reason for me to hide it from you, except that I was afraid you wouldn't want to be with me because of it. But now I want you to know everything. No more secrets. Ever. I want you in my life and I'm willing to do whatever it takes to make that happen."

Gabe looked over at the empty seat, the one that Cora had been sitting in before she went to use the bathroom.

"I don't know where this Brian guy is right now. Maybe he's getting you another drink or using the restroom or whatever." Gabe's green eyes met mine and his pupils dilated and constricted. "But I don't care. I just want you to tell me one thing. Can he kiss you like this?"

Gabe then placed his hands onto the top of my shoulders and knelt down. Without any hesitation, he brought his lips to mine.

It was the most electrifying kiss of my entire life. The passion in that simple act was more intense than any I had ever experienced. It was genuine. It was real. It was exactly what I needed. His touch brought so much relief to the turmoil I had been fighting ever since I had left his house that morning. I breathed him in, not wanting to break the kiss. His cologne, his musk, everything was the same as I remembered and all of it felt like medicine for my wounds.

I reached up and placed my hands onto his cheeks, feeling the familiar stubble that I had missed so much. We kissed for a long time. My eyes were closed, but I knew people in the restaurant were watching. Did I care? Not in the least. This was love. I had no doubt about that.

After a bit, though, Gabe slowly pulled away. I opened my eyes to see his green irises looking back. They were full of love and fear that I would reject him again. I melted in front of him.

"Gabe," I whispered. "I-"

"-You don't need to say anything," he said, cutting me off. "I'm sorry and I hope that you can forgive me. If you can't, then I guess I can understand. I can't force you. As long as you know how I feel about you, then at least I'll be able to live with the fact that I tried."

"Stop it, Gabe. Just stop." I brought a finger to his lips to quiet him as I got up from my chair.

I stood on my tiptoes and kissed him again. He brought his hands down to my sides and pulled me into him. I melted once more, as all of the stress and emotional pain fell away. I had never in my life felt such relief.

When we finally broke the kiss, I took a look around the restaurant. An older couple was looking over at us and smiling while a young couple out on a date gave us a thumbs up. It seemed we had garnered some attention. My face heated with a blush.

"Do you forgive me?" he asked.

There was really no decision to be made. Gabe was the one I had been searching for up until I met him, and Gabe was the one that I needed the entire time we were apart. It was always Gabe and it would always *be* Gabe. Nobody could fill that place in my heart and it had taken two months of separation for me to realize that.

"Of course I forgive you," I replied. "I don't usually kiss like that when I'm angry with someone."

Gabe's lips curled up into an unforgettable smile. He managed a laugh before fixing me with his gaze again.

"I love you," he said, reaching out and brushing a strand of hair from my face.

My heart lifted as he spoke the words. And without any thought at all, I repeated them back.

"I love you, too."

Gabe leaned in and kissed me a third time. He lifted me a few inches from the floor, spinning me around. When he set me down, he took a step back and looked at the empty table where Cora and I had eaten dinner.

"But what about Brian?" Gabe asked. "I can't imagine he's going to be too excited when he sees us like this."

I looked past Gabe, watching as Cora finally stepped out of the bathroom. She looked confused as she approached us.

"There's Brian right there," I said, pointing toward Cora.

Gabe glanced behind him to see Cora giving a goofy face while waiving obnoxiously. When he turned back, there was a priceless look of shock written all over his expression.

"I'm so confused right now," he said.

Cora made her way up and wrapped an arm over Gabe's shoulder.

"Hi there, I'm Brian," she joked, in her deepest voice. "You must be Gabe. Good to finally meet you."

Gabe frowned, his dark brows knitting over green eyes until his expression changed to one of understanding. "You're Cora, aren't you?"

Cora let out a giggle. "Yeah, you got it. But seriously, it's good to meet you, Gabe."

The tension in Gabe's body relaxed slightly, but he still felt like a coiled spring beside me. "Is Brian a real person?"

I couldn't keep the story going any longer, and I didn't really want to anyway. I didn't need Brian any more.

"No, Brian doesn't exist," I admitted. "He never did. I made him up so I wouldn't have to go on dates for my blog."

"So you're telling me that there isn't anyone else?" he asked, the tension slowly slipping out of him.

"That's right. There's nobody else. There *couldn't* be anyone else." I turned to face him, but looked at my shoes as I admitted the truth. "I made up Brian so that my readers wouldn't think I hadn't completely lost my mind over you."

Gabe kissed the top of my head and slowly drew in a breath of relief.

"That might be the single best news I've ever heard. You scared the hell out of me, Harper," he whispered. "But God, I'm glad I'm here right now. I never thought I'd be this happy again."

"Me either," I agreed, looking up at him. He pulled me into him, his smile lighting up my world as we held each other closely in the middle of the restaurant, with Cora standing patiently nearby.

The pain in my heart had subsided and was replaced with the tingling sensation of love. I cried, as Gabe held me close. These were tears of deep joy, though, not of sadness. In just these few minutes of holding Gabe, my sadness had become nothing more than a distant memory and my future was already looking brighter than it had in some time. He and I definitely had some things to work through, but for now, the aching in my heart had ceased. And in that moment, that was good enough for me.

CHAPTER 26

had been fairly sure that I would never see the inside of Gabe's house ever again, but now I was standing on the deck watching the ocean once more. Not that I was complaining, though. I was happy to be there. In fact, the view of the ocean with the sun overhead never looked so good.

"I'm glad you came over today. We need to talk. I'm ready to work through this and make things right again. But first, we both have to come clean with each other," Gabe said, leaning against the railing of his deck.

"Yeah, that's probably a good idea," I agreed. My palms were sweating, but I felt calmer than I had in weeks.

His surprise visit at the restaurant had happened just the night before and this was the first time we had really had a chance to hash things out. This conversation needed to happen. It had been a long time coming.

"Where should we start?" he asked. The breeze from the ocean ruffled his dark hair.

"I guess what I really don't understand is why you hid it

from me?" I asked, starting the conversation. "How come I had to find out about what you did for a living by accident?"

"I was afraid that if you knew I owned Kindling Dating, then you'd think I'd rigged the algorithms so that I'd come up in your search results," he explained.

"Well, did you?" I held my breath waiting for the answer.

"No, absolutely not," he assured me. "I filled out the same questionnaire that you did when I created my own profile on there. That was the whole point of me doing it in the first place. Bastian, Leo, and I wanted to see what it was like to actually be a client, instead of trusting the feedback from our users. I was the only single guy so I was volunteered. I had no clue what to expect. Then we started talking and I wanted to meet you. I wanted to see if the program worked. And then I met you, and the algorithms didn't matter anymore. You were the perfect one for me."

"You could have explained this to me," I said, crossing my arms.

"I *tried* to explain it before you left that morning, but you wouldn't let me." He shrugged and looked out at the horizon. "You didn't want to hear it and I understand. I should have told you everything right away so that you didn't have to find out on your own."

I guess I did leave that morning without giving him a chance, I realized. *Was it possible that I overreacted? Did my emotion get the best of me?*

"I'm sorry I left that morning," I said. "I was just really upset when I saw that you were using me for an advertisement."

Gabe reached forward and took my hand in his. "I *never* used those ads that you saw and I never intended to. Bastian had left those on my desk to try and convince me. The use of our relationship for an advertisement was his idea. I'm not angry with him about it, though, because honestly, he had the best intentions. He just wanted to drive more traffic to the site. He didn't consider how much it would upset you. I love the guy, but sometimes he's a little out of touch with people's feelings, you know? He wouldn't have suggested it if he thought it would have made you break up with me."

"So you never posted the ads?" I asked just to make sure.

"Absolutely not," he replied. "As soon as you left that morning, I threw away that paper and told Bastian that we'd never do anything of the sort, no matter how much traffic it brought."

I took a deep breath. "What upset me most is that you didn't tell me. If we're going to make this work, then we have to be open with each other. A relationship is built on trust and there can't be trust when there are secrets."

"I know. And I'm so truly sorry for the secrets. I would give anything to take all of that back, but I'm grateful to have a second chance," he said.

"So speaking of secrets, there's something I need to tell you," I said slowly. Gabe's brows came together. "The first time we chatted, it was actually my sister pretending to be me."

Gabe gave me a *say what* look. "Why would she do that?" he asked, obviously confused.

"Because she signed me up for the website without telling me," I explained. "When she saw how strong of a match we were, she initiated the process so I'd have to meet you."

"That explains why the chats were different than you were in real life." Gabe chuckled. "Your sister knows absolutely nothing about sports, does she?"

"She's got that footballs are brown and that's about it," I said. "But, the me you met in person is the real me."

"The person that I met that day at the restaurant is the person I fell in love with." He reached over and brushed a flyaway strand of hair from my face. "I didn't fall in love with you through those chats."

I cocked my head to the side and flashed a playful smirk as something crossed my mind. "Not to change the subject, but had you been reading my blog the entire time we were dating? I remember there was mention of my website on the mock up ad."

"Yes," Gabe admitted. "I looked you up after our first date and when I saw your blog, I subscribed to it. I couldn't help myself. To be honest, your writing is amazing and hilarious. I laughed out loud at all of your bad dates from the past. That was funny stuff."

"You little snoop!" I teased, as I pressed my fingers into his stomach. "I'm going to start calling you Nancy Drew!"

"Hey, I may be Nancy Drew, but at least I didn't create a fake boyfriend out of thin air," he clowned back, tickling me just above my hips.

"Hey, Brian was the best thing that never happened to me," I said between tickles. "I miss him so much. He never argued with me, he didn't dirty the house and he'd come and leave whenever I asked. He was completely at my bidding. Oh Brian, Brian! My love, where art thou?"

I couldn't stop laughing as I wrestled away from him and darted to the other side of the deck. Gabe chased me playfully over to the lounging area. When he caught up to me, he grabbed me around the waist and lifted me up, throwing me over his shoulder.

"Is that Brian I see over there?" Gabe mused. "Oh wait, never mind. It's just a shadow. I must be seeing things."

"You never know when he's going to show up, though," I squealed, as Gabe carried me across the deck. "He's big and buff and afraid of nothing."

"Well, let me know when you see him," he laughed. "I'll make sure to introduce myself. Sounds like he and I could be good buddies."

It felt so good to play and joke with him again. It was helping so much with the healing process of my emotional wounds.

I continued giggling as Gabe hauled me inside and set me down onto his overstuffed couch in the living room. Then he sat next to me, draping his arm over my shoulder.

"Seriously, though, Harper, I'm sorry about what happened." He squeezed me with his arm. "Truly, I am."

"Me, too. Those two months were some of the hardest months of my life," I admitted. "I really missed you and I'm sorry I didn't give you a chance to fully explain yourself that day. I was just upset."

"It's okay. We both made mistakes, but now we can move forward. I just want you to know that I truly care about you, Harper," he told me. "Like I said at the restaurant last night, no more secrets. I'm ready to start something amazing with you and I don't ever want there to be anything between us that feels like betrayal. I won't let it happen again."

My hands were all over him as he spoke. I couldn't stop touching him. I had missed him so much and all I wanted was to be as close to him as possible.

"Let's not let little things turn into big things. We can't allow stuff like that to keep us apart, ever again. It's just not worth it," I said. "How about right now, we make a pact that we'll be open with each other? I'll never make another blog post about our relationship without involving you in it and you do the same for me and your website."

"Deal," Gabe stated.

We held each other as we gazed out to the back porch, watching the sky turn a deep orange as the sun set. I closed my eyes and breathed him in, savoring the moment all that I could, grateful that things had turned out for the better.

"Out of curiosity, though," Gabe began, after a few moments of relaxation. "If we're going to be together, and you aren't going on any more bad dates and since Brian doesn't exist, what are you going to blog about?"

"I don't know." I shrugged. "I mean, I'm still taking reader submissions for bad dates and Cora is sending me plenty of material to publish on the site."

The blog hadn't been at the forefront of my mind recently, but as I sat there and pondered it, I realized that I wasn't as interested in it as I had been before. Keeping up with the website seemed to be more of a hassle than anything else and it wasn't bringing me very much joy any more.

"You know what? I'm not so sure where the website is headed these days," I admitted. "I'm thinking about it right now and a part of me is really considering handing it over to Cora."

"Seriously?" Gabe turned and looked at me in surprise. "I thought the site was your baby."

"It *was*," I agreed. "But I'm not so sure that it is any more. You brought up a good point and it made me think about what I could blog about. I'm sure I could come up with stuff, but for some reason, it's not really appealing to me right now."

"Maybe it's time to move on from it?" Gabe suggested.

"Maybe it is," I replied. "It's something to think about anyway." It definitely felt like a time for change, at least as far as the blog was concerned. "I'm thinking I might take some time off to do my own writing. Maybe I'll focus on writing things that I'm interested in."

"Like what?" Gabe asked. He began stroking my hair and I felt like purring with delight.

"I don't know exactly. Maybe I could write about traveling or shopping or something I really enjoy," I mused. "I can't get over this feeling that it's time for me to move onto bigger and better things."

"Do you think Cora would want to take over the blog?" he asked, his fingers finding magic spots on my head.

"I think she would love nothing more than to have full control of that site," I said. "She posts more content to it than I do these days, so really, she should be the one to reap any future benefits from it. Plus, she's not really happy with her current job."

The more we talked about it, the more concrete my decision felt. I was seriously leaning toward handing over the blog to Cora and letting her have a field day with it. She was still enjoying her awful dates and I was ready to move on and just settle in with my new boyfriend. It was the perfect situation to take the next step forward in my life.

"I'll call her later and talk to her about it," I said, as I snuggled up closer to Gabe. "For now, though, all I need to do is watch this sunset with you."

Gabe kissed the top of my head like he always did and it sent a pleasurable tingle into me. After two long months without communication, we had finally kissed and made up. I was surprised at how easy it was to repair things with Gabe. It shouldn't have been so easy, but I assumed that part of it was because of the sheer ridiculousness of the argument that had torn us apart in the first place. We'd both overreacted and let our emotions control our decisions. It didn't matter now, though. All that mattered was that we were finally back in each other's arms. I was safe and sound and my heart was at peace.

CHAPTER 27

The following week I finally sat down to prepare for my final blog post. My decision was made. It was time to say goodbye and pass the reins onto a new owner. It made sense and it felt right.

Gabe had told me to sleep on the decision, and for most of the week I had made my home at his house, which made sleeping *really* easy. But the truth was that it really hadn't taken much deliberation; the blog seemed like a thing of the past, something that opened the door to new writing feats, and I was ready to walk through that door.

During our time together I had allowed the blog to slip even further off my mind, which was entirely okay with me. I had checked in periodically and had found a quick selection for Worst Wednesday. But besides that, and for the first time in a long time, I hadn't paid it much attention. It seemed that the blog and I had finally begun to outgrow each other. At one time it had been my baby, but now it was moving out, and Cora was the perfect guide.

If there was anything that was gnawing at me about the blog, it was that I still had a mess to attend to. I had provided no resolution and not even a spec of news after my last post hinting at an imminent proposal.

After dinner one evening I called Cora to discuss the prospect of her assuming the blog, and even she had mentioned that my readers were commenting and begging for an update on Brian. It was like a mess of spilled milk sitting on the table, permeating the air and desperately waiting to be cleaned up, and I was less than eager to mop up the mess. *But they say not to cry over spilled milk, right?* I recounted the cliché and reminded myself as I finally sat down in front of my computer.

I was perched in Gabe's office and sitting in his chair that was so massive it hugged me like a cocoon. His office was lit by a single lamp and came complete with a bookshelf full of novels, computer coding manuals and a few textbooks. His desk faced west toward a large window that encompassed most of the wall. It looked out upon the swaying waves of the water and the sun that was nearing the end of the day.

I sat and stared out the window as I contemplated what my readers would want to hear and how I could align it with the incredibly improbable way that things had actually happened. Everything really had worked out in the most extraordinary way possible. The words in my last post were more ironic than I ever could have imagined; my life *had* twisted and changed drastically, and as I had ignorantly predicted for the sake of the blog, I would have *never* seen it coming.

It also felt ironic to be writing the post at Gabe's house, but I was more than okay with it. There was something oddly comforting about sitting in his confines to mop up my mess and move on from the blog. I could hear Gabe milling around in the other room, and inside I smiled.

The cursor had been blinking for several minutes at the top of the blank page as I sat there with an empty stare. I needed a way to reintroduce Gabe in a positive light so that I could naturally reference him moving forward. After all, if I was going to switch my focus to a different blog, there was no doubt that Gabe would be involved. Not only that, but his persona and our relationship would add to any future narrative I would write. I needed to devise a story in which Brian faded into the distance while Gabe came bounding in heroically. I continued to sit for a few moments before telling myself to just start writing. So I did.

Hello everyone! I am back with the news that you've been waiting for.

Well... I'm back with some form of news, that's for sure.

*Last time I wrote, I told you all to expect some exciting for the next post. I talked all about twists and turns and incredible surprises, and somehow in the midst of all of that rhetoric, I only managed to further mystify myself. I blabbed on about all these different kinds of **feelings** and intuitions, but even I could have never imagined what was in store.*

As I said, Brian and I went to dinner that night at my favorite spot in downtown Miami. It was good to see him, as always, but immediately I could tell he was acting a little weird. Something about him was just off. At first I chalked it up to 'one of those days' at work, but when I asked him about it, he assured me that all was well.

Our conversation seemed muddied and more

dull than usual. He even seemed to order in a mundane tone that I hadn't heard in awhile. I was beginning to get nervous. Could it be that after blissfully anticipating a proposal, I was sitting in the midst of a breakup? There certainly was the scent of a breakup in the air, and he wore it like cologne.

We ate slowly and I tried my best to enjoy the incredible food while also stressing the idea that this might be our last date together. After dinner, Brian left for the bathroom. He usually liked to order dessert and I sat there half looking at the menu and half imagining the last time a guy had used the bathroom as a method for escape. (I'm sure you all remember Mr. Bathroom, I certainly do despite trying my hardest to wipe the memory from existence.)

So there I was, sitting alone at the table and pondering how it is that I always seem to end up in a situation where someone feels like the bathroom is the best way to escape my company. But this time, I knew he wasn't just dodging the bill. If Brian had been tight on money, not only would he not have suggested such an upscale location, but he would have simply told me to pay and promised some form of 'compensation' later that night. He had already been gone longer than expected and had even taken his phone. My initial worry was beginning to turn into a very real fear.

I debated the idea of just leaving and avoiding the bad news altogether. I was starting the think that it was my turn to be the 'bad date' and pull *out a move from the miserable inventory I have accumulated.*

*I was beginning to come to terms with leaving and never talking to Brian again when all of a sudden, Mr. Perfect Match came through the door. You know, the guy that I had matched with online until our relationship crashed into a fiery pit of burning turmoil? Yeah, **that** guy came strolling through the door headed straight for my table.*

If I was debating running away before, it now seemed like the only option. If I had a jetpack strapped to my back, I would have blasted up through the roof of the restaurant and out into the Atlantic Ocean.

But Mr. Perfect Match approached and I was too paralyzed to move or even speak, so he spoke first. Immediately he began to spill his heart to me. Apparently he had been keeping up with my blog, and knew about Brian and our date scheduled for that night. Not only that, but my big mouth had hinted at a proposal, and he said he couldn't allow that to happen. He knew exactly where I would be when I said "my favorite place in downtown Miami," and he sat down in Brian's empty seat and told me that he wanted one more chance to try and rekindle our relationship.

Dear Lord my life is bizarre. You would almost think I was the mastermind behind a massive scheme to get Gabe back or something, but I promise you, I'm not.

I STOPPED and paused in the way that I always did when a thought in the back of my mind seemed to step out and tie my hands together. I was no mastermind, I knew that. And although it hadn't been my intention, there really was *no* name for what had happened. Even as I attempted to fabricate a story I felt like I was only coloring over a picture that was already in place. *Maybe I had masterminded Brian,* I wondered. But it was for the sake of my readers. I could never take credit for the way things had panned out. *I don't care if my readers think I'm a conceited jerk, it's time to get Brian out of here,* I thought as I began typing again.

 *Eventually Brian returned from the bathroom. His face looked unpleasant until he saw Mr. Perfect Match sitting in his spot, then it turned to sheer bewilderment.*

Mr. Perfect Match politely stood up and offered the chair back to Brian. But then he became real serious, and looked me in the eye and told me that I needed to choose between him and all the memories we had made, or a future with Brian. It was like I had gold in one hand but was offered the world in the other.

It was then that Brian announced that he wasn't proposing. He was actually going to tell me that he was transferring his job to Seattle and would be moving at the end of the month.

My choice was so easy that I knew fate was pushing me to make the right decision.

So here is some big news, although I know it's not the news that any of us were expecting. Mr. Perfect Match and I are back together, and we are exceptionally happy. It has been the reason that you've all had to wait so long for an update—and I apologize for that—but after talking over our differences, I now feel like I am back in a relationship that was never meant to end.

So there it is, and even after all of the unbelievably terrible dates I've recounted, I dare say this may just be the most unbelievable story of all. But oh well, what are you going to do? There's not much left to do besides be thankful for the way things concluded, and also conclude a few things for myself.

It is time to do a little bit of revealing. I'm sure it's obvious that I've always changed the names of the people involved in these blogs in the interest of disclosure. So believe it or not, but Mr. Perfect Match isn't in fact his real name. No, his real name is Gabe and he is incredibly smart, and wonderful, and every bit as amazing as I have described.

*Which leads me to my next topic. I want to also reveal and inform you all of a website called Kindling Dating. It's the website that originally matched Gabe and I and it's the reason for our happy union today. I'm not usually one for promoting dating sites, but it really is a tremendous website with a super friendly and simplistic platform. If any of you are into the realm of online dating, I **highly** recommend Kindling Dating. I truly believe it has the best pairing methods and algorithms out there. If it can find **me** someone like Gabe, I know it can work for anyone. Just keep in mind that sometimes it takes* *more than formulas and math, sometimes it takes a true chemistry ;)*

I'm just lucky that I had that chemistry with someone so spectacular. And speaking of me, beyond being the girl that goes on bad dates, I was actually given a different name on my birth certificate, and that name is Harper.

I am revealing all this information because I must also reveal that I will no longer continue my work on this blog. By now you are all familiar with my good friend Courtney Catastrophe who has been the one going on all the bad dates you read about over the course of my relationship. What a sacrifice she has made assuming the duty of dealing with all the boneheads out there. She has done a fantastic job and no doubt will continue to do so, so I urge you all to continue to keep up with her work and continue to submit your posts for Worst Wednesday.

MY EYES SHOT up from my computer as Gabe entered the room. He was dressed in cozy clothes for the evening and wore a smirk as he approached the desk where I was working.

"What'cha working on?" he said cunningly, for he already knew the answer.

"Just finishing up my blog," I replied and turned the chair to face him. He continued to round the chair until he was behind me squeezing my shoulders and massaging gently.

"Are you writing something juicy about me?" he teased.

I laughed. "Actually, I think you're going to laugh when you read this one. It took some time to think about a way to craft things and make them work out."

"You mean you didn't want to say that I showed up expecting to confront a guy who didn't actually exist?" His voice was full of happiness and it took everything I had not to turn around and kiss him silent.

"Shut up!" I said instead.

"It looks to me like you're crafting algorithms or something," he said, leaning forward and peering over my shoulder. "You know this is the chair where I did all of my most brilliant work?"

I couldn't help but laugh again. "Do *you* know that if you keep distracting me with all your super hilarious jokes, I'll never be able to finish?"

"I think you should take a break and come watch the sunset with me," he continued to rub my shoulders as he had done throughout the conversation. Finally I turned around to face him.

"I'll never be able to finish this thing if I don't do it now. It's already like a week late," I said with a thin frown on my face. "But I'm almost done, I promise!"

"Okay..." he said warily, "I don't know if you were planning on reaching up to grab the sun and stop it from moving, but if not you've only got a few minutes until we miss the sunset."

I looked out the giant window to the west. The sun wasn't quite setting, but Gabe was right, it was nearing the time.

"Okay, I'll hurry! I really will!" I promised him and he smiled back before leaving the room to allow me to work. I picked back up and began typing quickly.

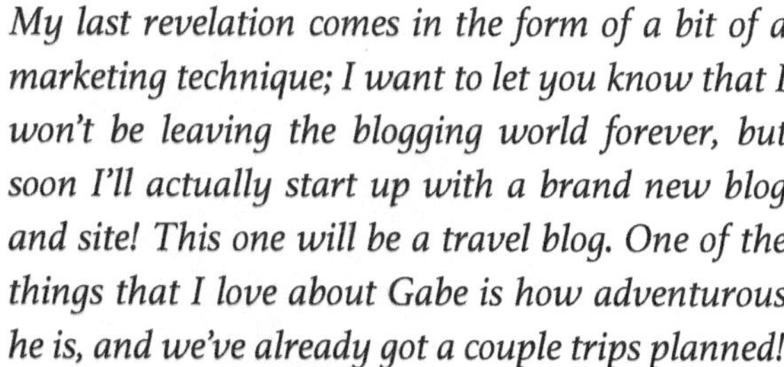

My last revelation comes in the form of a bit of a marketing technique; I want to let you know that I won't be leaving the blogging world forever, but soon I'll actually start up with a brand new blog and site! This one will be a travel blog. One of the things that I love about Gabe is how adventurous he is, and we've already got a couple trips planned!

At the beginning of next week we will be leaving for Jamaica! Neither of us have ever been and we're both extremely excited. We've got an exciting itinerary filled with beaches, jungles, waterfalls and lots of smiles.

I promise I won't sound so sappy in the actual blog, but it'll be fun to write (and hopefully to read) and Jamaica will be the topic of my first post. So if you're ever curious, please stop in and give it a read and subscribe if you'd like!

I HEARD something drop and the sound of shattering glass in the other room.

"Babe, are you okay in there? Did something break?" I called out.

"I was pouring us some wine but I think Brian knocked the glass out of my hand. He's probably still upset at me for stealing his girl," he yelled back.

His response made me stop and laugh.

"Did I just tack on another thirty minutes with that distraction?" he joked back.

"Oh hush, I'm almost done!"

"That's okay, maybe we can just plan to watch the sunrise or something," he said mournfully.

Again I laughed, though I tried to do so quietly so he wouldn't hear. I decided to pick up again immediately before I engaged and lost my momentum.

> *Well, here it is, I guess it's that time. It feels weird to be concluding my final post, but I guess every sun sets eventually.*

I PAUSED to look out the window at the sun and the water and smiled as I thought of Gabe waiting in the other room.

> *Now is about the time when I would say a temporary goodbye and ask for your hilarious comments, but I want to give you all one last comment of my own: THANK YOU ALL SO MUCH!*
>
> *You guys got me through a lot of bad dates, but even more long nights when blogging seemed to be the only thing that could tame my anxious mind, and you guys were always there for me. I've taken every one of your comments to heart and can't thank you enough for all your support along the way.*
>
> *So as I always say, bye for now! I really do love you all.*

I HAD TAKEN many final breaths after a long post, but this

was it, and I exhaled heavily as I skimmed the page and admired my final work. It was time to bid farewell to the blog, and if Gabe hadn't been waiting I would have taken a few moments to reflect, but instead I hit Publish and watched the blog as it posted.

It was bittersweet and while I hated to see it go, I felt terrifically light as the weight of the blog and all of its responsibilities finally fell from its rest on my shoulders. *Cora's going to do great with this,* I thought to myself. *Or should I say, Courtney Catastrophe.* I had originally told her that she didn't need to pick a name that sounded so forcefully cliché, but she had insisted. And she would continue the blog with the same sense of edge and attitude.

The sun was beginning the creep closer to the horizon and the water's edge. I dashed out from the office and into the living room where I could see the outside balcony through the windows. I could see two chairs pulled together with a table in between and a bottle of wine and two glasses waiting patiently, but no Gabe.

I already had Gabe's name on my lips about to call out when I felt his arms wrap around my waist from behind. I jumped.

"You scared me!" I said, still wired with adrenaline.

"Well, I've been *waiting!* Are you finally ready to go outside?" he asked with the smile of an eager child.

I wanted to tease and taunt him back after the way he had startled me, but instead I defered to my pleasant side that had been waiting to finally come out and sit with Gabe to watch the sun fall into the ocean waves.

I turned around to look him in the eye as he still held me at my waist. His hands were soft and his grip was comforting. I beamed into his bright green eyes and took a still breath before speaking.

"I don't think I've ever been more ready," I told him, placing my hands on his shoulders and drawing his lips near to mine.

Slowly, like the setting sun and the ocean horizon, our lips came together on his island. The soft scent of a tropical island, the waves, and the beach mingled with his cologne and I knew that I would forever be in love with his island kisses.

EPILOGUE

I never thought this day would come.

Maybe when I was a little girl, I had hoped that someday it would. But I never actually believed it. It feels like a dream, but I know it's not because it's even better than anything I could have dreamt up.

I'm marrying Gabe Honors. In just a few moments, I'll be wed to the love of my life.

I'm beyond nervous, but also ready. I've spent the last twenty minutes looking at myself in the mirror, making sure that my hair and makeup look absolutely perfect for him.

"Hey, it's almost time," Cora says, as she steps beside me. "You look perfect, Harper. Seriously, you look gorgeous. Gabe is going to melt."

I hope she's right.

"Well, let's do this," I said, trying to keep my voice steady. "I'm ready."

Just outside, my mom is standing there, holding my little nephew's hand. He breaks away and runs up to give me a quick hug before she tells him to go take his seat. Mom looks almost more nervous than I am. She can't keep her hands still and she's tapping her toes against the sand.

"You look amazing, Harper," she says. "My first born baby girl is finally getting married. I can't believe this day is finally here."

"Me either," I say.

"Are you ready?" she asks.

"Beyond ready."

"Good." She steps close and pulls me in for a hug. "I'm so proud of you. I knew things were going to work out for you. I can't tell you how happy I am."

For some reason, in that moment, it feels good to be held by my mom. She squeezes me tight and I feel young again. I flashback to when I was a little girl and she was the main focus of my life.

"I love you, Mom," I whisper.

"I love you, too, Harp." She kisses the top of my head and then holds out an elbow for me, walking me toward the ceremony.

Gabe and I had spent countless hours trying to figure out the perfect place for us to get married. We debated between a football stadium, a private island or the top of some high-rise tower in New York. They were all extravagant ideas, and would have certainly been memorable. But after a little thought, we agreed to something a little simpler, something a little more romantic.

The beach.

For most of my life, the ocean reminded me of childhood. But since I had met Gabe, the water only made me think of him. Our relationship is built around the water. We'd watched hundreds of sunsets together, admiring the sun as it sank below the horizon behind the ocean on his island home. The beach represents our love and so we eventually both agreed it would be the perfect place to get married.

When I look up, I see the rows of wooden chairs in the sand, with an aisle between them. I quickly glance over the audience, noticing mostly familiar faces, but a few I don't recognize. It looks like a sea of billionaires, all wearing expensive suits and dresses, immaculately adorned for occasion. My occasion. Our occasion.

When I look to my left, I notice that Bastian's wife, Ava, is in the audience. She flashes a smile and nods her head, as if to say "I'm glad Gabe found you". Gabe's other business partner, Leo is there with the love of his life, Charlotte. Charlotte already has tears in her eyes, which she wipes away with a handkerchief. In the front row, I see Jack and Emma, another pair of my new billionaire friends, with smiles on their faces that are even bigger than my mom's.

But even with all of these people here, when I look toward the front of the aisle, I no longer see them. They disappear and I'm left standing in the sand with just one man in front of me. He looks gorgeous as always, only today he's especially beautiful. He's dressed up in a black tuxedo. His jaw drops slightly when he sees me standing there and his green eyes light up, making the ocean behind him look drab in comparison.

I don't know how long I stand there admiring him. My mom squeezes my arm, and whispers, "Come on, Harper. It's time to get married."

I nod and walk beside her as she leads me toward Gabe. His smile grows with each step I near him, and the butterflies in my stomach release, bursting into a chaotic ball of energy and excitement, but mostly love.

"Who is it that gives this woman to this man?" the pastor asks.

"Me. I do," Mom replies, her voice trembling as she holds back her tears. Mom gives me a final hug and kisses my cheek, before making her way back to her seat in the front row.

"Dearly beloved, we are gathered here today to join this man and this woman in holy matrimony," the pastor begins. His *cadence is slow and steady before he pauses. "That's all I have to say, because this lovely couple has taken it upon themselves to bring their own vows. That makes my life very easy."*

The audience laughs at the pastor's joke and when they settle down, Gabe pulls a piece of paper out of the pocket of his suit coat. He looks at me and I feel everything he's feeling. The emotion and love is so thick in the air that my knees become weak.

"Harper, the first time we met, I fell deeply in love with you. I knew that you were the one I wanted to spend the rest of my life with. Every moment we have spent together since that day, my love for you has grown. My heart, my soul and everything that I am, belongs to you. You are the most amazing and perfect girl I have ever known. You make me happier than I ever thought possible and I feel truly blessed that you have agreed to be wife. So I make these vows to you in the presence of our closest friends and family, so that they may witness the promises I make. I solemnly vow that I will spend every day doing everything I can to be the husband that you deserve; to support, love and cherish you; through the happiest times, but also through the darkest times. I vow to be your best friend, your closest soul mate and, most of all, your faithful husband. No matter what life may throw at us, I vow that I will never stop loving you, will never stop caring for you and will never stop striving to be the best possible husband that I can be. I love you, Harper, with every single fiber of my heart."

I swallow back the tears as he finishes reading. My hands shake as I unfold my piece of paper to read my vows.

"Gabe. In you I have found my best friend, my confidant, my lover, my inspiration, my better half, my soul mate. You have already taught me so much about the kind of person I want to be. You love with your whole heart and soul and give all that you have whether it is deserved or not, whether it is appreciated or

not, whether it is returned or not. You are the strongest person I have ever met. No matter what life has thrown at you, you have been able to thrive and prosper. You have an amazingly positive attitude and your good humor is infectious to all of those you surround yourself with. I am far from perfect, this you know of course, but you accept me for who I am and love me for my flaws, not in spite of them. I know that you will always support me no matter what this life throws at us, even if you don't agree with me, which might possibly happen once or twice. I promise to always cherish you, honor you, respect you, be true to you and love you with every ounce of my being. You were meant for me Gabe. And I was meant for you."

I drop the piece of paper and it falls to the sand at my feet. I hear crying in the audience now and I wonder if my mother has brought enough tissues.

"Now Gabe, repeat after me," the pastor says, once the audience has quieted down a bit. "With this ring, I, Gabe Honors, take thee, Harper Thomas..."

Gabe takes my hands in his. He looks me in the eyes and I melt just like it was the first time I met him. He had me from that very first moment in the restaurant. I knew he was the one then and I definitely know now.

"...to be my lawfully wedded wife, to have and to hold, from this day forward, for better, for worse, for richer, for poorer, in sickness and in health, until death do us part."

Gabe repeats the words from the pastor. He speaks proudly as he does so. There's no nervousness in his voice. This is what he wants. This is what I want.

"Groomsman, please present the ring," the pastor turns toward Bastian, who stands nervously behind Gabe as the best man.

Bastian pulls a small box out of his pocket and hands it to Gabe. He opens the box in front of me and removes a beautiful silver ring with a single-set diamond in the middle. As he slips it on my finger, I lean toward him, wanting so badly to kiss him right there. I stop myself, though. It's not time yet. The best kiss of my life is coming and I have to be patient.

Once the ring is on, the pastor turns to me. "Harper, repeat after me."

The words flow out of my mouth as though my heart is speaking directly. I had been waiting my entire life to say these words and it feels amazing.

"With this ring, I, Harper Thomas, take thee, Gabe Honors to be my lawfully wedded husband, to have and to hold, from this day forward, for better, for worse, for richer, for poorer, in sickness and in health, until death do us part."

I slide the ring over Gabe's left finger, grateful to see it fits perfectly.

"Now, Gabe, you may kiss the bride." The pastor says with a wide smile.

Gabe steps forward without any hesitation. He takes me in his arms, leans in and gives me an electrifying and thorough kiss. I melt into him, and my heart feels content in a way it never has before.

He's all mine.

The audience goes insane. They cheer and clap. I can hardly hear anything at all. But I don't need to. When I look at Gabe, he mouths the words, "I love you". It's the only thing I need to know.

"I love you," I reply.

We kiss again and this time, the sound of the crowd drowns out. It's just us, Gabe and I on the beach somewhere. I have all I could ever want in my entire life: The most amazing man in the world and island kisses.

Escape With Me: A Midlife Love Story

"I gave it all up to be happy. I'd give it all up again for you."

They say life begins after 40, but Cassie ain't feelin' it. Divorced and feeling trapped by her job, she wants to let loose for her friend's tropical beach wedding. She decides to let her hair down and get a little unpredictable. That's when she meets a handsome bartender, Wyatt.

Despite a few grey hairs, Wyatt's the liveliest man that Cassie has ever met. She knows that there's got to be more to his life story than just being a bartender, but this is just supposed to be a vacation fling. And after sunny days spent breaking all the rules on the beach together, Cassie realizes that nobody has ever listened to her the way that Wyatt does.

His carefree life is enviable, his kisses are intoxicating, and she can almost imagine a life with him. But all vacations come to an end. And when Cassie invites him to visit her hometown, Wyatt reveals that he can never go back. Not to her town. Not to America. Not to civilization.

Cassie leaves, confused and heartbroken, wondering just who she got herself involved with. Suddenly, her predictable life gets turned upside down when she sees her picture splashed across the Internet. And when the tabloids come looking for the mature woman who found the lost billion-aire, she has no idea what to do...

...until he comes back.

Escape With Me: A Midlife Love Story

ABOUT THE AUTHOR

New York Times and USA Today Bestseller Krista Lakes is a thirtysomething who recently rediscovered her passion for writing. She is living happily ever after with her Prince Charming. Her first kid just started preschool and she is happy to welcome her second child into her life, continuing her "Happily Ever After"!

Thank you for supporting an indie author. Anything you can do, whether it be writing a review, or even simply telling a fellow reader that you enjoyed this, helps me out immensely. Thanks!

Krista would love to hear from you! Please contact her at Krista.Lakes@gmail.com or friend her on Facebook!

Further reading:

Bad Boys and Babies
Family Doctor's Baby
The Billionaire's Baby Arrangement
Crime Boss Baby

Kinds of Love
A Forever Kind of Love
A Wonderful Kind of Love
An Endless Kind of Love

Billionaires and Brides

Yours Completely: A Cinderella Love Story
Yours Truly: A Cinderella Love Story
Yours Royally: A Cinderella Love Story

The "Kisses" series

Saltwater Kisses: A Billionaire Love Story
Kisses From Jack: The Other Side of Saltwater Kisses
Rainwater Kisses: A Billionaire Love Story
Champagne Kisses: A Timeless Love Story
Freshwater Kisses: A Billionaire Love Story
Sandcastle Kisses: A Billionaire Love Story
Hurricane Kisses: A Billionaire Love Story
Barefoot Kisses: A Billionaire Love Story
Sunrise Kisses: A Billionaire Love Story
Waterfall Kisses: A Billionaire Love Story
Island Kisses: A Billionaire Love Story

Other Novels

I Choose You: A Secret Billionaire Romance
His Every Desire: A Billionaire Seduction
Wolf Six's Salvation: A Shifter Love Story
Burned: A New Adult Love Story
Walking on Sunshine: A Sweet Summer Romance
An American Cinderella: A Royal Love Story
Mr. Darcy's Kiss: A Contemporary Pride and Prejudice